T0196390

THE PRISON BOOK

A Novel

ALCOHOLISM/ADDICTION: A LIFE SENTENCE

TAMARA SEGARS OTT

ARCHWAY
PUBLISHING

Scripture quotations are taken from the Holy Bible, New Living Translation, copyright ©1996, 2004, 2007, 2013, 2015 by Tyndale House Foundation. Used by permission of Tyndale House Publishers, Inc., Carol Stream, Illinois 60188. All rights reserved

Archway Publishing books may be ordered through booksellers or by contacting:

Archway Publishing
1663 Liberty Drive
Bloomington, IN 47403
www.archwaypublishing.com
1 (888) 242-5904

ISBN: 978-1-4808-5572-4 (sc)
ISBN: 978-1-4808-5571-7 (hc)
ISBN: 978-1-4808-5573-1 (e)

Library of Congress Control Number: 2017919059

Print information available on the last page.

Archway Publishing rev. date: 12/15/2017

Dedication

For my husband Mark- the most wonderful person in the entire world. At least in *my* world—the one that matters. You are my favorite person, my rock, my lover and my *very* best friend. I have always known you are a precious gift to me, from God. Thank you for always believing in me, and never giving up on us. I love you, Baby.

For Mom and Dad. Thank you for your unconditional and everlasting love. You provided me with the best possible upbringing and opportunities a girl could ever ask for, and I thank you with all my heart. I love you both so much.

For my precious, precious sons. You'll never how much I love and adore you.

For everyone who has suffered, is suffering, and will suffer from addiction in any way, shape or form. Stay strong, and get help, please. It won't go away until you make up your mind to get rid of it. Resources for help include Alcoholics Anonymous, Narcotics Anonymous, AL Anon, your local community health center, and your state alcohol and drug abuse prevention coalitions.

For The Father, The Son, and The Holy Spirit.

...and for Bunnie Lou- God bless you, sweetheart.

EPIGRAPH

The Serenity Prayer

God, grant me the serenity to accept the things I cannot change, the courage to change the things I can, and the wisdom to know the difference.

Living one day at a time, enjoying one moment at a time, accepting hardship as the pathway to peace.

Taking, as Christ did, this sinful world as it is, not as I would have it.

Trusting that He will make all things right if I surrender to his will.

That I may be reasonably happy in this life and supremely happy with Him forever in the next.

Amen.

"Don't be drunk with wine, because that will ruin your life. Instead, be filled with the Holy Spirit… And give thanks for everything to God the Father in the name of our Lord Jesus Christ." *Ephesians 5: 18&20* The Life Recovery Bible. New Living Translation. Tyndale House Publishers, Inc., 2013.

"The trouble is with me, for I am all too human, a slave to sin. I don't really understand myself, for I want to do what is right, but I don't do it. Instead, I do what I hate. But if I know that what I am doing is wrong, this shows that I agree that the law is good. So, I am not the one doing wrong; it is sin living in me that does it." *Romans 7: 14-17* LRB

What does God want from us? He has a specific purpose for each one; believing God is essential for lasting success. He may intend to use us to bring saving grace into the lives of others who suffer from the same affliction. Recovery is part of that purpose.

As we are freed from our dependencies, we are ensured a life of good and healthy living. Our failures and mistakes graciously disappear, often to be forgotten. Moving ourselves from slavery to freedom is assurance God has a better life in store for us. Obedience to Him along with consistent love and respect are essential for our progression in recovery. Our journey can go from worse, to wonderful.

I believe we are all here on this earth to help each other get from this life to the next- people needing people. Use your God-given gifts to help others; encourage, listen, and speak.

"Don't let evil conquer you, but conquer evil by doing good." *Romans 12:21* LRB

"A final word: Be strong in the Lord and in His mighty power. Put on all of God's armor so that you will be able to stand firm against all strategies of the devil." *Ephesians 6: 10-11* LRB

I will strive to make every day better than the one before, therefore, the day I die will be the best day of my life. ...Tamara S. Ott

ACKNOWLEDGEMENTS

Thank you to the people at Archway Publishing.

INTRODUCTION

Marley Thomson Marx is an extraordinary person. Her amazingly striking good looks parallel her above-average intellect, and her compassionate, outgoing personality outweighs her appearance and IQ combined. Marley has one flaw- one enormous, deigning flaw of character -she is an addict; an alcoholic.

Raised in Texas in an upper-class, Christian family, Marley is afforded opportunities and advantages in life many people only dream about. She succeeds in almost every endeavor in which she puts forth even the smallest bit of effort, but at the same time struggles with the oppression of being drawn to the forces of alcohol addiction, and the evils therein.

A caring mother, loving wife, dedicated daughter and true friend, Marley, now middle-aged and imprisoned from the horrific results of her disease, looks back over the years and how her life has evolved. How did this nice girl end up in a place like this—not only this physical hell, but with the life-altering battles her chronic condition imposes?

The Prison Book's Marley Marx tells her story. She describes her accomplishments and failures, as well as a variety of instances she can never explain due to alcohol-induced blackouts. Her multiple relationships over the years include five marriages and many other pertinent, and not-so-pertinent people in her life.

This is the story of Marley, her *life sentence* as an alcoholic/addict, and her struggles to be free.

PROLOGUE

THIRTY DAYS IN THE HOLE… *Son* of a *Bitch!* I can't believe I'm here. My God, I absolutely cannot believe I'm here, in this pathetic, disgusting place!!! What have I done? Jesus, what have I done—to myself, my life, my family? Please Lord, let me wake up and this whole thing be a bad dream- a horrible, horrible nightmare. I don't belong here. Dear God in heaven, I don't belong here…in jail. Not in *prison*.

This wasn't in my plan: it isn't how my life is supposed to be! And certainly not what my parents wanted for me—their precious, beautiful, intelligent daughter—the one who always attended Catholic Mass. Not *me!* They raised me so much better than to be ending up here, in this dungeon, like a caged animal. Like a maniacal dolt separated from life, from the living. These people don't know me. I'm a good person. I help people. I've never hurt anyone; well, not with malicious intent, anyway. And if I did ever hurt anyone, it was always myself, so who's counting? Isn't that what is supposed to separate the good people from the bad, the things we do—our *intentions*? The evil people are locked up; they're the ones who are caged because they're like wild tigers preying upon the needy, the helpless and the unfortunate. I'm not that way. That isn't who I am. I help those less fortunate than me. I don't belong here. This place is for criminals—crooks, thieves, and murderers. I don't want to be here, sitting behind a steel door—a locked steel door. Between concrete floors and cinder-block walls, having to share a nasty toilet with women I've never even seen before, and certainly, by the looks of some of them and the way they're speaking and acting, I would never associate with them in the world. Some of them so disgusting the filth oozes from their pores, their mouths, their decrepit thoughts. That's who they are; not me. Trash of every race, color, and creed, and *anything* in between. Illegals and drug-fucking addicts, trailer scum—everywhere. And me. Even the guards are disgusting, and so fucking loud! God, make them stop yelling!

They treat me like I'm a serial killer, a murderer of mothers, or children. Handcuffs on my wrists, and shackles around my ankles, having to walk like an inchworm, the way they do in the horror movies and the crime shows I've seen on television. It's all so degrading, so belittling. Waking next to a mafia princess—more of a bitch from the minimal conversation, or lack thereof I've had with her—a street whore, and a child rapist. Oh, and I can't forget the couple of husband-killers across the hall. I guess they decided to kill their husband so they could be together. How disgusting. I'm not sure which is worse, killing your husband because he's an asshole, or because you've turned gay and so's your BFF. I've never had neighbors like these before, not where I come from. Not in my neighborhood; not in my lifetime. Oh, these poor people. They haven't a clue, no idea about life and how it should be. And here I am. God help us all.

"Shut up!" "Sit down!" "Don't talk!" "Hands behind your back; don't look!!" I have more respect for a foam-spitting pit-bull than I do for these gawd-damned imbecilic jackasses for treating me this way. If they knew me, the way I am—my character—would they treat me this way? Would any of this even matter?

Why didn't I stop? I sit here in these vile, filthy striped rags, surrounded by underachieving dolts; I'm so ashamed to be a part of this perdition. This existence isn't me. I'm happier than this; my life is… supposed to be. I have so much to live for, and to be proud of, yet so many things I should have done differently…

PART I:

CHAPTER 1

SISSY AND I RUSHED ANXIOUSLY through the long hallway, the clattery of our go-go-boot clad feet being heard on the wooden paneled floor. My long wavy blond hair bouncing to the beat of my steps; Sissy's dark shiny locks resting behind her shoulders. Mom kept the floors so clean; the two of us almost slipped into each other racing to see who would get to the 1960-something Rambler station wagon first. The area behind the backseat, cargo area I guess it was called, had an unattached carpet. Every time Mom turned a corner or drove over a bump in the road, we'd slide or go airborne. Can't believe I was actually that small; everything was big. Life was big.

"Last one to the car's a rotten egg!" Sissy always yelled, *after* she'd be ten paces ahead, toward wherever it was she was challenging me to go. Always ahead of me, wherever we went, whatever we did.

"Don't forget to tie your shoe!" I'd stop mid-stream, look down at my dirty-white go-go-boots and realize there was nothing to tie. She'd continue on to win the race; go through the imaginary finish line, this particular time being the backseat of the Rambler. Sometimes it was a door. She got me again. Always did. Don't all little sisters do what their big sisters tell them to do? Isn't that the way it's supposed to be?

Daddy had been waiting in the idling car for some time. He was always the first person in the car, last one out. Dads have it that way, you know. Always going first to get things rolling, or checking out a situation before calling to his troops it's safe to proceed. They're always the one to risk their life to save the wife, or drop the family off underneath the safety of a pavilion or porta cache', then drive off into darkness and light-ning, find some out of the way parking area to place the barge-on-wheels, and walk back to wherever the culmination of partygoers and strangers decide to gather. Usually it's a place he doesn't want to be, but when the event involves a kid or two of his, well, his attendance record tends to reflect perfection. Any aspect of tardiness can certainly be attributed to the current status and condition of the cement harbor. Anyway, he waits, often impatiently, to be further instructed as to what his next move will be. That direction always comes from the family head—Mom. At least that's the unspoken saying in most houses. Goes like this, *"If Mom's happy, we're all happy"*. Happens in the best of families!

The Rambler was the color of an elephant's tusk, sort of ivory-looking. The more I think about it, the more I loved that car. It looked like a mu-tant pearl, fresh out of a clam's shell—a prehistoric dinosaur-sized clam's shell. At least that's what I saw when I looked at it. Shiny and pretty like that, too. One day I opened the kitchen door to go outside and play, and the Rambler was gone. Some big gaudy Chevrolet station wagon had taken its place. Looked like a big blue tank. I was mortified, like I'd lost an attachment to myself or something. For a while, I mourned the passing of the Rambler—felt like a damn death to me.

"Come on Anna Belle! We're going to be late!" Daddy yelled. I could see the corner of his eyes as he looked over his black-rimmed glasses—the same kind Gregory Peck wore—toward the house. He didn't sound like he usually did in everyday talk. His mouth didn't move much, as if his jaw was nailed shut, tight. As I look back over the years, seems when I'd hear Daddy say that, I'd usually say quietly, sometimes to myself *"Come on Mom!! Let's go*!" Things were not going to get any better at this point.

Mama was in Bubba's room, trying to finish dressing him. His new cowboy boots were obviously a struggle, what with his feet the way they were. He had to wear braces for a short while—his feet pointed in the opposite direction his legs directed them, kind of looked like ducks' feet. Until he figured out we were going somewhere. Mom always had a time with Bubba's shoes cause of his feet, or possibly because Bubba was a little shit, and she always struggled with whatever it was she had to do with him. He sure was a cute kid though, sort of looked like Donald

Duck—had real cotton-like blond, almost white hair, and his little lips sort of protruded like a duck's beak. Cutest thing you ever saw. Maybe *that's* the reason Mama never could get him dressed and ready in a timely, calm fashion.

They came from PayLess, the boots did. Most of our shoes came from Payless; sometimes from Ward's or Grant's. Sissy always told nice old ladies her pretty smile came from Grants'. The only thing I remember getting from there was white cotton underwear. Granny panties I call them now. Still the same look, just bigger.

Bubba *hated* riding in the car. Absolutely loathed it! Once he figured out we were going somewhere in the car, he pitched a gawd-awful, ear-aching fit. As much as I loved to ride, he hated it, and I'll be damned if he almost ruined my fun every time. As soon as the car started rolling, Bubba began to scream and cry out at the top of his lungs. Reminds me of when people get on a roller coaster for the first time. Once the ride starts, they shut their eyes and scream the entire time, until the ride comes to a complete stop. Sometimes Mama would threaten Bubba, and tell him that she was going to stop the car and let him out if he didn't stop all that hollering.

"Mom, aren't you going to let him out?" I'd holler at her over his yelling, reminding Mama of her threats as we were stopped at a red light. But she never did. *Did she hear me? Was she ignoring my reminding plea? Probably not. Well, yeah, probably.* Why she didn't just reach over and slap the shit out of him is beyond my comprehension. The hollering stopped when the wheels did, every single time. I had to learn early on to tune out the noises which were making me anxious and uncomfortable. Didn't know it at the time, but that's what we do when we're young; we learn to cope in the most primitive of ways. Whatever works. Guess that's when I started riding in the back of the car, sliding around on the throw-rug in the cargo area. I suppose Bubba's actions and crying wasn't all for the bad after all.

~✝~

The very moment we were in sight of all the beautiful, sparkling lights, my heart would race; pound so fast and hard like it was going to explode right through my chest. I felt as though my body was all giggly inside.

Wow! There it is! Look at all the lights! And the giggles would pour out of my mouth like milk pouring into my cereal bowl. The bright lights were of every color imaginable. There were colors I never saw before! Some were dancing up and down; others turning 'round and 'round. There were lights flickering off and on, and I was headed straight toward them.

The fair—my favorite time of year, well, besides my birthday. But Christmas was one of my favorite times, too. And I loved Halloween; dressing up in some cool costume then going door-to-door, trick-or-treating. There was always so much candy!! Easter was always such a pretty time. Mama and Daddy looked so glamorous, and I always got a brand-new Easter dress. Sometimes Mama would take us to a lady who'd make Sissy's and my dress. I don't remember what Bubba wore. I guess he had something special, too. We'd go to the lady's house a few times before Mama would let us bring the finished product home. Once Sissy got stuck by a needle stitched in the hem of her dress; Mama never went back to that lady's house. In fact, I don't think we ever had our own personal seamstress after that. "She attacked me!" Sissy wailed. Absolute assault on a child they'd call it today.

I loved painting the Easter eggs. We'd sit around the table on Holy Saturday, dying the multiple dozen eggs Mama boiled that morning. In the later years, they came out with decals and color-sticks that would make designs on the shells. I just liked all the pretty colors, mostly. Our Easter basket would be filled with all sorts of neat goodies on Easter morning. The Easter Bunny had come! Sissy and Bubba and I eventually learned to look behind the chairs in the living room when we'd wake Easter Morning. That's where they'd be. It was almost as good as Christmas Eve, when Santa would visit the house. Oh, and summer. I loved summer, too!

~†~

Daddy always bought us corny dogs and cotton candy. Oh, the smell of the fair food, like no other aroma in the world could match. Just walking down the midway isles was a competition for the senses. My nose would be experiencing ecstasy in an aroma-orgasm when I'd catch eyesight of all the thrill-seeking rides; the music of the carousel, the screams of the teenagers on the bigger rides. And the ponies; oh, the precious ponies walking round and round. They never looked happy, though, and I could sense it. With their heads down, they'd walk slowly, dreadfully, as if they were walking to their demise. Sometimes I felt that way when I saw a kid mounting for a 4-circle turn. I'm sure sometimes the pony would rather be walking out his fate.

After consuming massive amounts of delicious junk food and a whirlwind of frills on a few rides, we'd adjourn to the rodeo in the large pavilion. We had the same seats for years and years, damn near the best ones money could buy. But I don't think ours were bought; Daddy always cut a deal with the fair-man, that's what I called him. The Fair-Man. He was a gentle soul, always smiling. Daddy and he had business dealings, that's how we always got the good seats. One of those "...*you do good for us, and we'll do good for you...*" sort of things. Totally legit. That's the *only* way Daddy rolled.

A few feet away from the gate where all the gallian horses and their equestrians entered the massive arena, I'd sit on the edge of my seat, wide-eyed and feeling as though I was the Queen of England at a Knights' event. I can recall riders galloping in on their steadfast creatures, always seemingly a smile on his or her face, and mine was always the first one they'd see- the only that mattered as far as I was concerned. My heart beat pounding right along with the pace of the evening. My smiles were ear to ear. I had that big smile like Audra on *The Big Valley*. And long hair, too. Always thought I looked just like her, until I was about seven, maybe eight. That was the entrance to the awkward stage. There was nothing awkward about Audra. Yes, I was the beautiful star of *The Big Valley*; the Queen of England at the rodeo. No longer the cowgirl princess. And Daddy was the guy who got us special favors from the Fair-Man. I suppose when I'd brag to my friends about our special treatment, I wonder now if they might have thought Daddy sold candied apples, or was a clown or something. Probably. I don't know. But that's when I fell in love; my first true love. Horses. I made up my mind then that I, too, would someday be riding my own beautiful steed.

CHAPTER 2

MOM AND DAD NEVER WERE "drinkers". I honestly believe I can count on one hand—maybe two—the number of times they've actually drank an alcoholic beverage. They just never cared for it, that's all. I remember they'd get all dressed up—Mom in an elegant long dress, sometimes sparkling—usually leaving the house with her lovely full-length coat with the fox-fur collar, and Daddy, so dapper-dazzled in a black tux and those shiny leathered shoes. I never understood the funky thing that wrapped around his waist, though. Like a belt, but it wasn't. Guess men sometimes try to figure the reasons for us women wearing the stylish get-ups we do, though. Anyway, on this occasion have a hi-ball before the fairy-princess whisked them off to the ball in their carriage made of a pumpkin- that's how I imagined it- and we were always left with a babysitter. Mama and Daddy never went out much, so we never had a regular babysitter. But once it was a real old lady. She fell asleep shortly after my parents left, and I thought she had died. But she hadn't. I was glad Mom never made us stay with her again. Probably I was more pissed off because she fell asleep in my favorite rocker; well, the only rocker, but it was the unstated *my* chair. Another time, we had a teenager—Suzie from down the street—stay with us. The next time Mom called Suzie to ask her to come watch us, she told Mom she had a date to study with her boyfriend, but that she'd come over if she could bring him. Mom and Daddy didn't go out that night, and I never saw Suzie again.

Another really special time of year, the only other one when Mama and Daddy got really spiffed-up to go out was at Christmas time. It was for a major event, a gala from Daddy's work—a convention ball of some sort, always in some big city. Houston, maybe, or Dallas. *Road trip!* Sissy and Bubba and I always got to tag along, and as soon as we walked into the elaborate hotel's lobby, I imagined myself as an aristocrat of the finest; a movie-star on location, or some good-looking man's exquisitely-adorned wife, with diamonds and fancy cars. The bellmen were always my servants as my chauffeurs waited for me to make the call, whatever that meant at the time.

The days' events would be a schedule of meetings for Daddy and Grandfather. This often ended up a family event, since so many of my relatives—the men—were in the same type of business. Mama and the other wives would attend luncheons and other social events such as meets & greets, stuff like that. So that left the kids to come up with our own activities. Of course, Mom always knew exactly where we were, usually at the ritzy hotel's pool, or at the tree-lined park close by. One year while Bubba and Sissy and I were at the pool, we watched a group of older kids enjoying themselves with all sorts of things the poolside waiter kept bringing them- burgers, drinks, ice cream. The waiter would bring a tray full of delicious-looking taste-tempting items, then give the tall kid a piece of paper to write something on, then he'd leave the good stuff with the kids. Bubba decided to do that one day, and I could hear Daddy yelling at him later that night from down the hallway as I was coming back to our room after riding the elevator. I had gotten bored, and decided I'd ride it up and down, and up and down. I told Bubba not to do it.

There was a lady in the elevator who looked like Cruella Deville, and she gaped at me as if I had done something wrong. If I didn't know it then, I would certainly know it now. I had been riding down one elevator and when it reached the lobby floor, I'd change over to the next elevator and ride up to the top floor, change and do it all over again. At some point in my excursion, I ran into *her*, literally. Cruella at her most evil. Her wicked stare towering 10-feet above me scared the daylights out of me, so I decided to take the stairs to our floor instead. Cruella had ruined the thrill, and as I was walking back to our room, I heard the hollering coming from the other side of our hotel door. Not good, not for Bubba. And not for me, I was thinking, if I choose to go in there. Didn't want to take that chance and get more bummed out than I already was, so I decided to go see what Grandmother and Grandfather were up to. They had the coolest of all the rooms. It was on a spherical side of the hotel, overlooking a beautiful roundabout on the street, making me feel like I was in Rome next to the Coliseum. I called theirs the Roman Coliseum Room. They were always fun to be around and never got mad at me. I knew I was safe with them.

The big night had arrived, yet the evening was young. Tonight, the night of the ball, I would be able to sit at the spot of my choosing, and gaze at all the beautiful ladies in their lovely ball gowns, armed with their prince-charming as they proceed to a night of elegant grandeur. The orchestra would play while couples danced the night away, forgetting that realities of life existed. And Mom and Dad would bring up some weird-looking thing they'd claim they won as a door prize.

But before all of that, I would sit in the Room of the Romans, and enjoy with Grandfather what he always called his "happy hour". He made his bourbon and Coke, and would allow me a sip. He'd take one. I'd take one. Grandmother didn't know we were so into sharing; she was busy trying to make her face look years younger with the latest in cosmetic ingenuity, although Grandmother was beautiful as she was. Then she'd stroll to the balcony where Grandfather and I were perched, and help herself to his tasty refreshment. Highball—they called it. I liked it, and I was feeling fun, again.

Sissy, Bubba and I sat in our room watching television, *The Brady Bunch* and *Bewitched*, I remember, while the extravaganza went on downstairs. Mama had ordered room service, and we ate like little pigs off a large silver tray brought to us by another young man in a weird-looking outfit, like the waiter at the pool that day. Before leaving for the evening, Daddy looked at Bubba, "And stay off the phone", he demanded.

Bubba was a strange bird; he screamed bloody hell when riding in the car. He had to rock and roll his body maniacally from side to side, just to get to sleep. So much so that if any live being had a nose or eyeball within arms' distance of Bubba while performing his ritual for sleeping, they were sure to walk away with a broken nose or black eye. Strangest thing you ever saw. Lil' Bubba slept for hours that night. He was a late-night lightweight.

~✝~

The evening was lovely. Crisp, cool southern air with a dash of breeze here and yonder. The sky was lit by the near Winter's moon and glowed from what seemed to be a trillion dancing stars, twinkling everywhere I looked. And off in a distance the city lights reflected over the treetops on the horizon. Daddy told us that if we stayed away from the balcony, we could keep the sliding door open, so we pledged our vows. But with the openness of the night, for some reason watching *The Twilight Zone* after midnight was creeping out Sissy and me, so we elected to change the channel and watch something more soothing and a bit more uplifting.

Shortly thereafter, Mom and Dad walked in. Albeit they were not arguing, I could tell there was an unpleasant tone in their voices during what seemed to be a very disjunctive conversation.

"Stay here with the kids, and I'll go down and see what I can do to help," Daddy said to Mom, and he made his exit from the room.

At that moment, a terrifying scream came from the direction of the balcony, along with the sound of a "splash". The three of us—Mama, Sissy and I—trotted over instantly to see what the commotion was about.

"Oh my God!" Mama screamed.

"Mama!" I responded.

"Is he dead?" demanded Sissy. We all were looking at what we could tell was a man's body, floating face-down in the large hotel swimming pool, several floors below. The lights in the pool reflected the beautiful aqua-colored water, as the shimmers of it reflected off the hotel's windows and ornate concrete walls. All of a sudden, the body came to life, as the man began splashing water with his hands, jumping up and down the way a toddler does when it's play day in the pool. Then the man exploded with a roar of laughter which echoed in the hollows of the hotel's design.

Had he jumped in the pool from his balcony below? Did he just decide to take a swim in the middle of the cool December night, with all his clothes on, and when the pool was supposed to be closed? What was wrong with him? Was he crazy?

I looked over as I saw a shadowed-figure walking quickly toward the pool, alongside others on their way to rescue the madman. The shadow was my father. Then I looked over at Mama as I heard her say something. She was looking up at the starry sky, quietly uttering under her breath, "Oh dear God".

"Let's go in now, girls", she said sadly, sort of gloomily, as she turned to escort Sissy and me back into our room.

"Mama, is that Uncle Frank?"

"Yes honey… It's Uncle Frank."

CHAPTER 3

BRIDGETON WAS A "DRY" TOWN in the late 1960's, although back then I had no inkling as to what that meant, nor did I care.

Sometime between that of the fun-filled nights at the fair and the glamorous-evening escapade, I rode with Daddy on a Friday night to a little glass building out on a small two-lane highway. Daddy held my hand as we walked in, and told me to be careful not to touch, or break anything. The place was filled with bottles of every shape and size, which held all sorts of colorful liquids. There were posters of people having fun on the beach; pictures of beautiful girls in scantily-clad outfits laughing as they were holding some of the bottles I was seeing as we walked the tiny isles. The man at the counter asked Daddy if he could help him find anything in particular, and I remember never having heard the response he was given. Then I saw another poster; that of some really cute guys laughing as they were playing something—kickball or soccer—in a parklike setting. They were holding some of the cans I was seeing in the store's nearby display.

Daddy paid the man at the counter, and picked up the small brown paper bag claiming the glass prize. I was just happy to be riding along that day with my Daddy. The trip back to the house was long, and we talked about one of his favorite topics—football. I didn't know much about the sport—still don't—but I liked spending time with Daddy. I enjoyed listening to him talk about something that sparked his interest. Some Autumn days I'd sit on the couch next to him and pretend to be enjoying what we had our eyes glued upon on the television. I guess I was really enjoying myself because Daddy was enjoying his game. Mama didn't agree with his favorite pastime; she didn't see the meaning of the sport, and usually let it be known. But I was there to lend encouragement. And I've sometimes passed by that little building we drove to that day, going to and fro. It's dilapidated and closed now, but it makes me reminisce of simpler times long, long ago.

That Friday night in particular, Mama was in the kitchen cooking dinner. I asked her if I could help. At that age, I suppose as long as I was in the kitchen making conversation with Mom, I was helping enough. She loved for me to be near, and I liked the duties of kitchen-assistant, usually having something to do with the newest in cooking gadgets. We always had the latest in whatever Ronco was selling at the time. Mama would summon Sissy and Bubba and me around the kitchen table sometimes on a day Daddy was at work, and we'd lick green stamps. Then we'd take the books of licked stamps to the green stamp store, and come home with all sorts of neat stuff. The house was filled with lovely items from the stamp place. Actually, the blender Daddy was using was a green stamp gadget. He poured in it the stuff from the bottle we'd bought that afternoon, along with a can of frozen stuff he retrieved from the freezer.

Daddy poured the pink concoction into a couple of the glasses Mom had bought with the stamps. This particular set of dishes looked like amber pineapples. My parents still use some of those dishes to this day. Amazing. The Slurpee-looking refreshment made my eyes tingle, and I asked if I could have some.

"You can have a little sip, Marley", Mom guarded as if she were facing off with a menaced burglar her prize possessions. *Sip my ass!* After one taste, I was on a mission. I wanted the entire glassful, and that in the blender as well. This shit was better than any Slurpee I had ever had from the corner store, and I waited until the family was adjourned in the living room later that night, watching the man I was going to marry, *Hawaii*

5.0-Man. Yes, I was in love. But not even Jack Lord could compete with the luscious pink purpose of my mission. I made my way—several times that night—to the refrigerator that housed the daiquiri in the amber pineapple glass. I didn't know why my head was feeling so good, but I was liking it, a lot.

CHAPTER 4

ALTHOUGH OUR FAMILY WASN'T GROWING in numbers, the three of us kids were growing in size. Mom and Dad decided we were outgrowing the small 3-bedroom clapboard home I knew and loved so dearly. Not only did they want each of us to have our own bedroom and more living space all around, they wanted us in the best possible schools, which naturally meant being in the newest and most opportune part of town.

Over by the lake, new subdivisions were making their way all over the tree-covered vacant properties, and that's where we needed to be. At least that's what they said. There was a new mall in that area. It leased department stores, a record store, a couple of restaurants and specialty stores offering the newest in fashions & fads.

But I wasn't going anywhere, and furiously! *How could they decide to move without asking my opinion first?!* I had just finished the best school year of my life- the second grade. I was the teacher's pet, and I loved my neighborhood and all the "gang" of friends I had for blocks around. No, I wasn't going anywhere.

One hot July night as I was finishing a marathon bike ride through the neighborhood, I saw Mom standing on the front porch, and decided it was time to let her know my stance. She replied, "Well, Marley, I hope you and that nice man will be very happy here together, because he just bought the house". As she spoke, she looked toward a guy in a black leather jacket, driving off on a motorcycle. *O.k., so maybe the new house won't be so bad after all.* I spent the rest of the evening packing.

~✝~

We seemed to adjust to the new home nicely, but I was finding myself being lonely at night having to sleep in a room without Sissy. I usually ended up in her bed, or she with me, at least for the first few weeks. But I gradually began to overcome the isolation when I realized I had my own space to decorate to my heart's content.

The record store at the new mall let me take home the life-sized Donny Osmond statue, probably because I bought one of every Donny Osmond poster they had to sell, as well as one or two of the Osmond Brothers. And I'm sure it didn't hurt my chances of acquiring the five-foot cardboard figurine when I took home Donny's latest Greatest Hits tape- the one that I constantly played on my new eight-track tape player. Daddy built some wall shelves for Sissy's and my new rooms, and I set the tape player on one of the shelves, along with so many of my horse figurines and other girlie stuff. I was quickly getting used to the idea of independent living, and liking it a lot.

That same year, my grandparents had decided to move up in the world as well. We met them- along with some of my aunts and uncles and cousins- one cold, snowy afternoon at a vacant lot out near the lake. There we stood, a sodality, a communion of relations around a large clump of dirt, and I was wondering why Grandmother seemed so happy as she looked at the dark wet mound. There, Grandfather would soon begin to build her dreamhouse—*their* dream home.

The following Thanksgiving kicked off with the christening of the beautiful brick mini-mansion. With the warmth and glow of a roaring fire in the large fireplace, the ambiance throughout the new palace was perfect for the enormous group of relatives to express and share familial love and gratitude for life. Even our favorite Priest stopped by to have a bite of turkey, enjoy a cold one and engage in our holiday cheer.

Holidays of every kind were always a joyous time for our family to gather and catch up on each other's latest ventures or just the local gossip. Everyone seemed to express their opinion on life's most recent challenges- some more so than others. And as the aroma of smorgasbord items filled the air, the volume level of one voice above the other seemed to always be rising.

While the sports fans gathered near the fireplace in the large television room, the others convened in the formal sunken living room, where the huge windows overlooked the vast wooded areas bordering the lake. And the teenagers in the house usually gathered outside in the backyard's large patio, where we could sit for hours, rain or sun, near the shady oak trees and discuss school happenings, new cars, boyfriends and the latest in pop-news and music.

For the next thirty years, this is where I'd spend special occasions of every kind— holidays, birthdays, anniversaries, and just great times. It's also where I'd learn to be the mistress of margaritas, a bartendress of sorts, and no one would ever give it a second thought.

For those very few who engaged in an occasional celebratory spirit, I took note at the built-in wet bar, of what and how much was measured and combined. I learned at a very early age that adults like their cocktails freshened up, and I became the master at hostessing this particular duty. As I went around the house extracting the half-empty glass for a pre-occupied relative's refill, to me, the glass was half-full, and that's all I needed to bring back that *neat, strange sensation* I had experienced before.

CHAPTER 5

FOR THE NEXT YEARS, SCHOOL would prove to be a close ally to me. Teachers seemed to always dote on me because of my academic excellence and outgoing personality. When the time came for students to be elected on their creative talents, it was my poem winning first place, to be published in the school's newspaper and cited at the annual PTA program event. It was my elaborate Crayola drawing showcased in the hall's foyer for the coming year where the encased read "This could be YOUR work this year". Amazing opportunities, and I seemed to *always* delve into them with half-force, and taking the prize of every win.

For a couple of years out of a few, I was formally invited to summers at what was called "Enrichment" school. This was a time for straight-A'ers to be singled out amongst the community; a chance to let their skills and talents shine abundantly through. A time when students who excelled in their everyday responsibilities of being a kid growing up in the all-American household to be honored, acknowledged and boasted upon by parents, and hated by siblings. Yes, loathed to the core by a sister and brother who seemed to always accuse, "You never even study!!" Well, I cheated. *Just kidding.*

I was the five-star kid, the protean child, the All-Star. Oh yeah, I was that, too. Even in extracurricular activities I won out on the All-Star teams and was the coach's favorite pitcher and first base girl. My success never wavered. Never, or so it seemed. Life wasn't just a gift, it was mine, and I was a gift to life.

By junior high—I believe they call it middle school these days—I was gearing up for the teenage years ahead of me, and the challenges and excitement heading my way. No disappointments there! One day I just happened to be rehearsing my role in the school's play (oh, did I fail to mention it was the lead role, the *title* role?) as I heard my name being called over the loud speaker. All of sudden screams were coming from every which way in the school's halls. I could hear the echoes of laughter riveting throughout the entire school: the ecstatic wails of others' jubilation. I had triumphed, once again, over so many other young ladies who had tried out for the oh-so-desired position of being our school's representative, of being cheerleader. Me. Cheerleader. It was the first of four years I would represent my student body and our school in this way. Once again, I sought and I won.

The 1970's brought some fabulous times to my young teenaged life, and fashion and style engulfed a designated section of my heart. Bell-bottoms, hip-huggers and knee-high boots were the rage, and I loved every stitch of it all. At 5-foot teen inches and legs up to there, it's no wonder why I always felt comfortable in the chicest of stores. The catwalk would soon become a very familiar place for me to spend my time, as I became a modeling fashionista for the most prominent stores in town. Up and down the runways in the latest of fads I strutted my stuff, loving every minute of it. But having this kind of fun at such a ripe, innocent age would prove to be nowhere close to parallel that which would become a 20+ year alcohol and drug-induced career in the limelight. Look out high school, here I come. Or I should have thought, *Look at me.... high school's coming.*

~†~

Over the next few years my life saw as much diversity as there are cultures on the planet. It soared like a stealth bomber from kid-hood to prime adolescence. I was the ever-so-popular beauty queen and representative of my haughty-taughty high-class school, and was gaining drastic popularity with the upper-class students., especially since I hung out with Sissy much of the time. It didn't take long for me to be inducted into the upperclassmen's high and almighty status- that which the lower classmen long to achieve over periods of time.

Bridgeton High had the reputation of being an upscale, state-of-the art educator's dream, and with my overabundance of versatility and enthusiasm, I could fit in with any group of kids around. I was kind, outgoing and friendly to everyone, never made a judgment call, and others seemed to reciprocate in kind. I began my time here with a pinch of naivete' and innocence. But life as I knew it was about to take a drastic turn.

CHAPTER 6

THE PARTY SCENE IN THE late '70's handed out an open invitation to a newcomer- me. Disco was a ball of fire with divas such as Donna Summer and Sister Sledge hovering over the pop music charts. Hit after hit was rolling off the tongues of The Bee Gees, and nightclubs were the places to be- young adults and teens clad in colorful satins, ruffles and all sorts of frilly things. And the shiny silver, glimmering disco balls made it all come to life on any night of one's choosing. Disco-dancing was in, and I loved moving to the music! And hand-stamping- WOW! What a concept. Get my hand stamped, go outside and enjoy a few hits off a joint, a swig of this or that- *and that*- then go back in to dance the night away.

Rock-n-roll was at its all-time greatest with fantastic hits from Fleetwood Mac, The Rolling Stones, Boston and Journey. Aerosmith, The Eagles and Pink Floyd certainly were not left behind, to name but very few. This was without a doubt the greatest age in music- for my ballot, anyway, and for my chosen genres.

Though Sissy and her friends were only minor years ahead of me, our mentality saw a definitive gap in maturity status. It seemed like a given that I'd fit in with the older crowd, the way some of my buddies did with their older siblings. But other than superficially, such was not the case. It just wasn't.

I began experimenting with marihuana—pot if you will, or weed as some call it—and immediately developed a grave fondness of the herb. I soon ingested the notion that no good party was complete without it.

Matter of fact, I enjoyed the high so much that I began to think no good *anything* should go without it- *that along with the variety of alcohol I was consuming.* I liked it- a LOT! Besides, pot was cheap and easy to get. Trash can punch and a joint would make for a really good time. It's just that I thought I should *always* be having a really good time. The bond between me and substance was in 3rd gear, and I was on the entrance ramp of the highway to hell.

I never had a problem attracting members of the opposite sex. I have *always* been popular with the guys. With my stunning looks and captivating personality, it was a no-lose set-up, I guess. I was dating a bit now, and that meant boys with cars. Boys with cars older than me, and coming from places like other schools. Times—they were a changing. I was having a blast and my friend-base was expanding ferociously.

One night after dancing the disco scene at an incriminating age, I found that possessing a fake ID was definitely a benefactor that afforded me times not regularly available. I went home to find that I had telephone messages from four different young men. Young men I'd seen at the club and who did NOT get my name and number from me. Hell, I was having so much fun dancing on the lighted colorful floors to the rhythm of the beat; I was oblivious to the fact that *anyone* was remotely interested. I loved to dance; I loved music, and I really didn't have any particular guy(s) in my crosshairs during that time. But I was indeed flattered, and selfishly impressed.

Over the course of the next few weeks, I went out on dates with all four gents—not at the same time, of course. Gary was a really nice guy. He wanted to be a dentist, and was very mannerly and proper. We went to an expensive steak house, and dined as if we were about to get married. Gary talked about his intentions for "us" and plans for life. Too much for me. He didn't drink, anyway. OK, we could be friends.

Johnny wanted to travel the world before even thinking about go-ing to college. He had a black and gold T-top Trans Am, and he was a handsome doll, but didn't have a clue about much of anything. He was fun, and sure was cute! I really liked the car. He traveled over the course of the following summer, and often wrote me, or called. He also told me his song to me was <u>Angel Baby.</u> He made me feel special, and I always thought of him when I heard that song. Pretty song. When Daddy met him, he was immediately NOT impressed. Johnny was a few years older than me and always looked stoned. Probably was. So, he was never invited back to the house. Johnny and I smoked some pot now and then, threw back some sauce and remained friendly over the years. I recently heard that he died a long time ago.

Some other guy, Dan, I think was his name, was as sweet as he could be, but showed very little assertiveness. *You can't get very far just being sweet, Dan. Plus, it gets boring after a while.* But, we were friendly over the next years. Never had much in common with Dan. He was just way too sweet. Sort of *oozing* with sweet. Not a good prospect for my demands.

So now we come to Brad. Wow! Brad was a movie star's man. He was very tall, like 6'2" —great height for my amazon build. His hair was black as night, and his smile was Colgate white. And his ass was squeezie cute! I remember our first date. He wore Window-paned jeans, sort of fashionably torn, with a dressed-up tank-top that showed off his tanned biceps and forearms. His body engaged the eyes in an orgasm of delight-sight, and his sex-appeal weighed like a ton of bricks on the personality scale. Did I mention we *really* got along? I found myself talking to him for hours at a time on the phone, until Mom insisted I get off the phone to let Sissy or Bubba, or even her use it. *How could she?*! She even mentioned the fact that someone might be trying to reach us. *Are you kidding me? That's ridiculous.* Brad had a Marlon Brando-style, revved up ride—something from the 1960's era, and it was bad to the bone. He was cool, his car was cool, and we were cool. We had definitely become an *item.*

Brad and I loved to "party". We liked smoking pot and drinking, but one particular time he engaged me in much too much drinking, and I experienced my first full-fledged drunk episode—one I will never, never forget. I was never so sick in my entire life. With a fifth of Vodka and many of the generic orange and strawberry sodas one can buy at any grocery store, we drank ourselves into oblivion.

I remember having a good time that night, feeling the euphoria that's set off when alcohol mingles with the brain's dopamine. But then all of a sudden, it's the next day, a Saturday, and I'm in my parents' room, lying on the bed. Literally crawling to and from the bathroom, puking my guts out over the commode, in what seemed like eternity. I think the Angel of Death was trying to pay me a visit that day—I was actually wishing for it. Mother never knew I had gotten drunk. I suppose because vodka doesn't give off an odor. Just vomit. That's bad, and I really don't know what she thought: she never said anything about it other than me being disgustingly sick. The entire day was one from fucking hell. This particular episode made the time I had Scarlet Fever in the first grade seem like a common cold. To this day, hearing the name "vodka" makes my stomach turn summersaults, and I'm not a gymnast.

CHAPTER 7

NOW, OFFICIALLY IN THE MIDST of my high school years and loving every minute of it, life was feeling really good. Being the student-body representative, cheerleader in an enormous 5A school, and enrolled in all accelerated classes, I was on top of the world. Brad and I had been dating for about a year, and we were pretty damn tight. Good thing was, he went to another upper-end school, so I was free to enjoy escapades with all *sorts* of friends, without being glued to one guy. I dated other guys, but Brad and I were always a pair. And when I hung out with him, I was always making new acquaintances—and some really good-looking ones at that. I actually did develop some lasting friendships with kids at his school—and some lasting, uh… other relationships. (Had I been ten years older, these relationships would be known as "affairs"). Hey, we were young and *not* married…yet.

One of the grandest parts of my teenage years, and a very fortunate circumstance that I can boast about was that my family was a member of *both* country clubs in town. Mom and Dad had joined one for our immediate family, and my grandparents had joined the other for us grandkids, and their social status in general. These clubs sat on the banks of the Bridgeton Lake, and were side by side. Only the most fortunate kids from the wealthiest of families belonged, and I spent much of my time there swimming, attending dances, dinners, and engaging in a variety of summer and year-round activities specifically designed for teenagers like me. We had two boats parked at one of the club's harbor, and when I said I took my friends out for a good time, boy howdy!

My family had a houseboat and a ski boat. Brad was always taking out his family's ski boat, and many of my friends' families owned houseboats and/or ski boats as well. Many years I spent enjoying water activities- swimming, skiing, sunning, eating- and of course, partying. When it was just us "kids", the ice chests were filled with MD-20/20 and Thunderbird wine, malt liquors of various brands and pot. Always pot. Most times were fun in Bridgeton, but summers were the atomic bomb! We were living the life of luxury, at its finest. Of course, school work came first if there was any, otherwise Mother made sure our duties and responsibilities at home were fulfilled before we could be leisurely, but I didn't have any complaints. Life was good, and I was a lucky young lady.

Sissy was away at college but was coming home for the weekend as my "Sweet 16" was approaching. We all gathered at Grandmother's for the special event, and I was sure I was going to get a large present with a huge bow. Yes, I got a car. A really cool two-tone brown, sporty Gremlin. I named her Gretta. Not to sound like a spoiled brat, but after Sissy got a car for her Sweet 16, I knew my turn was inevitable. And so, it was. After being blindfolded and led to the large, residential parking lot Grandmother and Grandfather had in the drive, there she was, just sitting, shiny and oh-so-inviting fun times for the future. I wasn't surprised, howbeit, I was truly excited. I "oohed" and "awed" as I jumped up and down with exhilaration and enthusiasm. Now that I had a car of my own, I wouldn't need to borrow other people's when I wanted to go to lunch, or skip classes. Did I mention life was good?

I had my own wheels, and I was cool as a cucumber. My Gretta was the new party-wagon and because of that I'd eventually turn my precious baby-doll into a rag-doll. In hindsight, Mom and Dad probably lived to regret the day they agreed to allow me to have such an expensive, freedom-inspiring gift at such a young age. But, as humans, we usually realize such things *after the fact.*

~✝~

My extracurricular activities were taking me all over town, and my modeling career had soared like a bottle-rocket. I now had an agent who was keeping me busy with fashion shows year-round, photo shoots for newspapers, catalogs and other print ads, and I was even interviewed on several area and statewide news and entertainment programs. I even did a commercial which showed on MTV once, but that would come later. With Bridgetown being an actively social and commercial city, I often was asked to play hostess at conventions and various events such as auto and boat shows. I was having an absolute blast getting out and meeting crowds of folks, strutting my stuff, exposing my potential as a someday professional, and getting paid all the while.

The school principal often let me skip school for whatever "modeling" job I was to be involved in. My grades were good, and I was an upstanding student in our community. I was responsible when I needed to be, and she liked me. Ms. Black like all her kids, mostly. But I, well, I was *special*. Always.

Liquid lunches were as much a part of school as class was, and since I certainly couldn't go back to school after drinking my lunch and with eyes as red as a fire-engine, I'd go to one of the many lake parks and hang out, or over to a friend's house where we'd listen to music, or smoke more dope. Sometimes we'd go to a rival school's parking lot while everyone else was in school, and I'll never tell the things we'd write on windshields of some of the "unfriendly" bitches' cars. We had fun. Lots of fun.

~†~

Living in Bridgeton was awesome, although everyone always said they wanted to get the hell out of there when they grew up and had the chance. I was no exception. But, it was home, and one of the advantages was that it was so close to the other big cities in Texas- Austin, Houston, Dallas. There were always great events like concerts going on, and it was nothing to cruise to an event and be home that night, get enough sleep and be on time for school the next day. And taking a road trip on the weekend was even better. *Way-rad!*

Expanding my horizons in other cities meant doing the same for my substance use. From my first concert (Molly Hatchet and April Wine, I believe) on, I began experimenting with pills such as Black Mollies, Purple Hearts and Yellow Jackets, whatever the hell all that shit was. Speed, if I remember correctly. Somebody would say "take it", and I would. Dumb. Real dumb. Like I mentioned earlier- hindsight.

For my seventeenth birthday, Mom and Dad gave me tickets to see The Stones, ZZ Top and a bunch of other bands. Course, Mom handed me the tickets and said "Happy birthday, honey. These are from your Father and me". Daddy never knew what the hell "they" were giving me.

I'd always hug him and say, "Thanks, Dad! This is great!"

Then he'd reply with something like, "Huh? Oh, you're welcome sweetheart. What'd you get?" I always laughed at that.

Anyway, it was an all-day concert at Dallas Stadium, and Sissy, my best friend Kerri and me had a blast! Sissy drove, and we smoked a joint before we even left town. Stopped by the best donut shop in the land, JJ's, and loaded up on a dozen donuts—*each!* Those were gone before we got to the concert. That was a day I'll never forget. We had a blast; saw a gazillion people we knew on the highway going there, at the concert, and on the way back. Stopped and got stoned a couple of times. Somebody brought along a cooler of alcoholic refreshment- I'm not sure who it was or *what* it was. Road trip! Party on Garth!

CHAPTER 8

THE 1980'S BROUGHT THE ERA of the "Hair Bands". Van Halen, White Snake and RAT were going strong; Loverboy, Poison and Motley Crew were just a few of my faves. Music was rockin' and good times with my plethora of friends were growing like wildfire in a dry forest. Discotheques had turned in to live rock clubs, and Brad and I were going strong, as were our attitudes toward sex and drugs; rock-n-roll had already established its claim on us. Brad was a raging hormone revved up for action, and I was along for the ride.

The catwalk had memorized my swagger, and my name was synonymous with some of the most popular department stores around. I represented style and fashion; I was chic. It was nothing for a fellow-student to approach me during class in the fall and let me know that over his summer vacation in a faraway state, he had seen my pictures on posters or in catalogs at a fashion mall. One rumor was that I had even made it to the casinos in Vegas. *Impressive!*

One year I was flown to California for several days to hostess a convention and pose with the event-goers for pictures, as I was the girl in the brochure. I was asked to go to Acapulco to do the same, but Mom and Dad didn't like the idea. Mom never flew, and Daddy never took off work. I would be going alone, and they said I'd need a chaperone. Needless to say, I wasn't happy with that decision.

I remember one commercial in particular. I was the young lady advertising a statewide gentlemen's fitness club. It was totally legit. But just for men; women have them, too. I guess the advertisers figured men would come flocking to the persuasion of a gorgeous young, tall blond insisting they needed to better themselves by working out, thus becoming members.

We traveled for the commercial, filming in different locations throughout the state. We filmed for hours in what would end up a couple of minute-long ads. It was grueling, but fun. Because we had to shoot in one of the clubs after hours, the event turned into an all-night party fest. Since the producer wanted to make sure we were all relaxed and at ease, he had plenty of booze and pot on hand for cast and crew members alike. Far be it from me to offend anyone being so hospitable, and paying me a good lump of cash as well. And since it was an all-nighter, there was plenty of cocaine to go around, especially for the striking blond star the producer had his eyes on. Nico wanted to make sure I was alert, and looking lively, especially after the effects of booze and pot.

The drive back to Bridgeton with Nico in his Maserati—or maybe it was a Porsche—was fun and exhilarating, until I repeatedly turned down his demands to go home with him. I was tired and wanted to go to my home; he insisted we go to his. Obviously, this is when the party ended and his ego deflated; it also voided any future commercials we had made a verbal contract to do. The only other time I saw Nico was when I went to his office to pick up my check. He gave me one last offer, and I said "No." I turned around and walked out. I *was still* the upstanding person I was raised to be, with good moral values. At least I didn't compromise *everything* I did. That's what I thought.

With all the glory and opportunities that were mine, the age of seventeen brought with it a level of rebelliousness I -nor my parents- never knew existed. Life was a constant party, and not always a happy one. I was testing all waters with Mom and Dad, and it seemed as if I was starting to drown. Staying out past curfew, coming in all hours 'round the clock reeking of alcohol and smelling of God knows what all, was not the sort of behavior my parents approved of. And regardless whether I was sneaking out of the house or back in, being caught straddling my bedroom window sill—one foot in the house, one foot out—did *not* make for pleasant conversation between myself and the arresting parent, and especially if I was supposed to be grounded. Having privileges taken away from me was becoming my new normal, and I wasn't game for playing by my parents' rules. Often times when Mom and Dad were asleep, I'd push Gretta all the way down the driveway, and start her up as soon as I passed their bedroom window, not giving a damn one way or other if they caught me *after* the fact. Once I was gone, that was it, and having to face my parents' wrath later seemed ions away. Hmm, maybe I'd die that night and never have to face then again. No worries there! Living for the moment, and every moment was about having fun. Rebellion was the topic and I was writing the book.

CHAPTER 9

DADDY IS A SMALL-TOWN GUY from the deep South, and my paternal lineage defines the term "good ol' country folk". They enjoy church functions, country fried foods and hot summer nights on the front porch. And every now and then they enjoy a nip or two of homemade rye called "moonshine". At least that's what I've always heard.

Personally, I never saw Maw-Maw and Paw-Paw Thomson take a nip. Maw-Maw was the sweetest of ladies in town, and she sure loved her grandkids. She was always baking some sort of fruit cobbler or crunchy creamy chocolate this or that, and she *always* cooked the freshest vegetables, taken right from her their garden. Many times, she'd have Sissy and me help her gather okra or purple hull peas food from the garden while Bubba tinkered with Paw-Paw on his machines; he was a mechanic and could fix anything that rumbled, mumbled or *grrr*-ed. Paw-Paw was a balding man with a paunch belly; he reminded me of Fred Mertz.

Maw-Maw told me of a story or two where she'd get downright furious with Paw-Paw from his days of moonshine-making with his cronies. Apparently, he'd indulge a bit more than she had allowed, and that kept him in hot water for a while, but he'd eventually mosey on back to the old drawing board, or to the cellar, I should say. Dixieland folk made distilled beverages quite a bit back in the day, and although so many did it, rarely did they talk about it in open conversation. Liquor was hardly sold anywhere but you could certainly get it from your neighbor's basement.

-+-

With the problems growing at home, Mom, Daddy and I decided we needed a break from each other; me from the folks and the folks from me. I seemed to be breaking every rule ever made in our household, and drinking and drugging had a tremendous amount to do with my behavior. We decided I needed a different environment for a few weeks during summer break, and when Mom took me to the bus terminal, I couldn't have gotten on that bus faster unless I was Samantha Stephens twitching my nose. I was headed seven-hundred miles away to my grandparents' home in the Deep South, and looking forward to the change in scenery, and of course spending time with my far-away, extended family.

If that bus stopped once, it stopped fifty times! *Jeez*, we stopped at every one-horse town along the way, and picked up and dropped off people constantly. But that was all right; I was able to secure me a great seat way at the back of the bus, and I quickly found that all the cool people sat back there. As the day turned into night, it was getting easier for me and my new acquaintances to take turns smoking pot in the latrine. People were going to sleep, and there were less chances of getting caught. Also, when people are constantly going in and out of the bathroom, it makes it hard to take turns smoking. We were having a really good time getting to know each other, and seems we all had our own personal stash- mine was in the ice chest I brought along with me- of alcoholic refreshments.

There was one nutjob, though, who really freaked out a lot of us as he began to speak in what sounded like tongues, gibberish. Although I have never experienced anyone doing this, when I saw and heard him, speaking in tongues was my immediate thought. During the wee hours of the morning while some people were sleeping, others were reading quietly or listening to their Walkman, this idiot began saying shit in a way that was truly foreign. He was talking to someone who wasn't there, while looking directly at the seat beside him. That seat was empty. Sleeping passengers began waking up, and the readers put their books down. Even the bus driver was checking out this weirdo in his large overhead mirror. Things were getting scary, and the faces of those around me were showing it, mine included, I'm sure.

The driver ordered the guy to be quiet and sit still, as the nut was now beginning to move about the bus in a radical sort of way. The bus driver radioed the bus in front of us, and then directed us to the approaching truck stop, where we pulled over quickly. The driver then demanded the escort of the dolt, who exited quickly and began circling the bus while flailing his arms, still yelling things no one could understand. The authorities arrived quickly thereafter, and took the maniacal nitwit away. What a weird, frightening experience. Somebody nearby mentioned the guy was from New York, heading that way, or something of that nature. He was certainly on something I've never tried, and definitely not interested in doing so. I've always enjoyed a certain feeling of euphoria, but insanity was never the goal. The driver received an ovation from us all, and we were soon back on the road, again.

I arrived at my destination, and Maw-Maw was there to greet me with hugs and a smile. It was nice to see her, and really nice to be off that damned bus. We spent the next few days catching up, cooking, riding around making acquaintances of old and shopping, Naturally, she and Paw-Paw weren't savvy to the mounting problems at home, but that wasn't necessary, anyway.

I remember one afternoon after church, we gathered on the lawn to meet and greet the local townspeople. I was introduced to a nice, attractive lady who reminded me of my Mother. *I was actually beginning to miss her.* The lady introduced me to someone even *more* attractive, her son, who, by the way, just happened to be about my age. *Good genes certainly run rampant in this family*, I thought to myself. He and I began conversing; he asked if he could give me a call, and I said, "Sure." I think his name was Randy, or maybe it was Daniel. Whoever he was, he was a college student in the neighboring state who'd come home for the summer.

Later that week, after a long hot day at the local pool, I headed to the casa for a nice home-cooked Southern meal and some quality time with the folks, when the phone rang. It was Randy Dan, and after talking a while, we decided to try out luck at getting acquainted, so we made a date to go out for dinner, and that we did.

We went to eat at some family diner near the state border -we weren't far from it anyway- and drove around looking at the beautiful scenery. Huge, tall pine trees with the smell of evergreen amongst the reddest clay dirt I'd ever seen; it was a beautiful place to be. Our musical tastes were similar, so that went well. I was sort of dreading the possibility he'd make me listen to some hillbilly jamboree shit or bluegrass something-or-other.

Randy Dan pulled out a joint and I was suddenly really digging this guy. He wasn't only good-looking, but he liked to party, too. *This might not be such a bad summer after all.* He liked me, too, I could tell. *Uh, yeah.* But then, while I was enjoying our scenic drive, we pulled into a dirt driveway, and up to a drive-thru window AT SOMEBODY'S HOUSE! Who the hell has a drive-thru window in their home?! This was weird, really weird. Oh, moonshine? That's what we were after. Ok, not so weird, just *strange.* Very strange. Definitely a *first.*

While Randy Dan placed his order, window-boy looked me over devouringly. Images of the movie <u>Deliverance</u> began racing through my mind, and I was glad when we were handed a couple of bottles and drove away. *That* was weird.

RD and I ended the evening drinking moonshine and smoking dope at his parents' beautiful home on some secluded ritzy golf course, and I tip-toed into my grandparents' house peacefully early the next morning. No harm done, no catastrophes. I said good-bye to Randy Dan, and we never talked again. I suppose the night wasn't so good, after all.

The time had come for me to go back to Texas, and the drive to the bus stop was a somber one. Maw-Maw always cried when watching any of us go, and I hugged her and told her I'd be back real soon, perhaps for the coming holidays. *God love her.*

I chose two seats at the back of the bus- one for me and one for my ice chest. The moonshine wasn't bad, and I made sure there was a to-go bottle in-tow. Comfied up in a window seat, I reminisced about my trip and what the near future may bring. The time was bitter-sweet, but I was soon making new acquaintances and enjoying the moment, traveling across the countryside, being "just me", and living for the moment.

Laughter was spreading in the back part of the bus, and the volume was definitely growing, and to my knowledge no one ever complained, except the bus driver when he pulled over in Pine Bluff, Arkansas. I remember because we stopped right in front of the high school, home of the Zebras. He stood up, and looked directly at the few of us in the very back.

"If I have to tell you people in the back one more time to be quiet, I'm pulling over and you're all getting off this bus!" he demanded. Well *dang!* For the next few hours you could have heard a pin drop. The thought of being stranded in the middle of the Ozarks interested us, NOT! We continued to enjoy the day, but in a very quiet sort of way.

CHAPTER 10

MOM AND DAD ISSUED AN ultimatum: either I go out for Varsity cheerleader and make it *while* bringing up my slacking grades, or they send me to private school FOR MY SENIOR YEAR! Oh my God! *Are you kidding me*? This was NOT going to happen, so I did, and I did, and they didn't.

I continued a heavy-scheduled modeling career, a busy extra-curricular schedule being Varsity Cheerleader, and my grades were sort of back to normal. I was in the accelerated classes, and even tried to work. The past couple of years I had worked odd jobs during the summer; I worked as a lifeguard at the waterpark one summer. So did my best friend, Kinsey. We were the tannest girls in town at the beginning of school, but we were drinking booze and smoking dope- along with who knows what else we were ingesting while doing so. We also were in a horrible wreck one night, which left a lot of people hurt, and that ended a lot of things, especially our friendship. Both sets of parents forbade us to see the other, but we did remain friends over the years. I always loved Kinsey. We were good friends, but not good for each other.

That year I was elected Queen of Homecoming, and was escorted to mid-field in a beautiful, brand new convertible Mercedes-Benz, by a gorgeous guy from the local university. (My outfit was absolutely stunning; I had recently modeled it in a fashion show, and bought it at a great discount. I especially loved the matching hat.) The night was spectacular, and I was truly a beauty queen. Life was good, again, and I was on top of the world.

The last year in high-school means parties, social events and turning eighteen- the legal limit to drink. Not that I hadn't been doing so all along. It just meant that I could do it *officially*, and use my own ID to do so. Though I was a regular at the clubs, I could now be there legally. One time I got pulled over for something really stupid like an expired inspection sticker, and I *accidently* showed the copper my fake ID. Uh oh! That cost me a trip to the City Police Department, and a night in jail. OK, so it wasn't all night, but a few hours in the pokey seemed to me like an all-nighter at the time.

Graduation meant total freedom, and it was just around the corner. But before that came the *spring break trip from hell*! A bunch of us loaded in somebody's car, and headed for the coast. Freedom, yeah! It was actually Mom and Dad's gift to me for graduation; they were probably as excited to get rid of me as I was to be rid of. And although Brad and I were still dating, he was finishing his first year at State University, and I was off on a week-long party.

All the usual drugs and then some, and more fucked-up people than I've ever seen in one place. One guy got so loaded he picked up a huge easy-chair and threw it right through a 3rd-story sliding glass door of a rented beach house. I actually got scared for a moment; he was *totally* fucked up on shit I never experienced, and I wasn't liking what I was seeing. I don't know who owned the house, but I guarantee they were some pissed-off people when they arrived and found out what all had happened.

Anyway, the people I was going to ride home with had an argument- I remember the girl having a fight with her boyfriend, and somebody got pissed off at somebody else, and a couple of us ended up without a ride. We hitchhiked with some other students; in other words, we got a ride with some other kids we really didn't know, but they were from a different school, and had to get back to Bridgeton when we did. Thank God, they were there, and I had the balls to ask around for a ride. It was either that, or ride the damned bus, and I didn't want to go through that scenario, again. Wild week if ever there was one!

Senior Prom was just around the corner, and I went with a guy who was a good friend of mine. He was actually one of my favorite liquid-lunch buddies over the years. His name was Mort. I'm not sure where Brad was, but obviously he wasn't around to take me. Possibly he was at State studying for finals; at least that's what he probably told me and I guess I believed it.

Nevertheless, we drank our asses off and smoked what seemed like a pound of weed, and chose to go on a river cruise before the dance. We certainly weren't going to the dance early; you know I always have to make a grand entrance.

"What the hell?!" I questioned as Mort was trying to escort me off the boat. Everyone was exiting, and I couldn't figure out what was going on. "I thought we were here for a ride up and down the river, right?"

"We *already went* up and down the river, Marley, for the past hour and a half. You've been talking the whole time," replied Mort. Wow. *Blackout.* Not good. If for nothing else but I don't remember having a good time. That's a bummer. Anyway, we continued on to the dance, got our pictures taken, danced to some Zeppelin and Foreigner and a whole lot of other great music, and ended the night however we ended the night. Whatever else we did remains a mystery. A couple of parties, I'm sure.

~†~

"The result is positive, Ma'am," said the lady in the Tweedy Bird scrubs.

"Are you sure? Please, please check again." I was begging for an answer other than what I had just heard. *Damn!* I wanted to die just then.

I was in the prime of my senior year, and no way was I about to let this happen. Well, I guess it did, anyway. An unwed mother, a child out of wedlock would *never* be accepted by my family; not *my* Mom and Dad.

Brad was doing great in college, and my plan was to go the opposite direction—not because of him—to attend a specialty school for my modeling career. I had it all worked out, and was really looking forward to a life in the big city with a career in fashion and travel. We had talked about marriage, but wanted to get through the next few years of school before we talked about it further. Immediate marriage plans were not in our future, and *especially* not one with a kid.

I had been on the pill, but when had I forgotten to take it? Had it been on one of those crazy nights I hardly remember? Why hadn't Brad ever reminded me, damn him. What about *his* fucking responsibility? Had we been *that* careless, *that* irresponsible?

Both of us skipped school that day, and I told Brad to wait in the car as I stepped in the beautiful, peaceful church my family had been going to since I was a small child. As I knelt down, praying for God's forgiveness for what I was about to do, tears of sadness rolled down my cheeks. Brad drove me to a clinic over 100 miles away, and we held hands the entire time there, and back, never uttering a single word.

PART II:

CHAPTER 11

GRADUATION HAD COME AND GONE, and I was finally a free bird! Though I had made my arrangements for the coming fall, Brad was begging me to move closer to him; he didn't like the idea of being so far away from each other after all, and I *did* have a lot of friends in that small, college party-town. Did anyone say "party"?!

As much as I was intrigued with the idea of going to the big city and expanding the horizons of my career, Brad's offer was sounding awfully tempting. After all, we were young, and they say "you're only young once", right? He wanted us to live together, but State had some old-fashioned rules about shacking up together, and to get assisted living we had to be married. Weren't we eventually going to get married, anyway? And I wasn't ABOUT to live in a dorm, what with sorority bitches and rules, rules, rules. I had just *left* rules. So, we planned a pretty large wedding in a pretty small amount of time, walked down the aisle and said "I do". It was a beautiful wedding, actually. Brad later told me that when he looked down the aisle and saw me coming toward him, he had never seen anything so beautiful in his life. We were in love, young, and now married- in a *college* town.

A week before school started, we spent our honeymoon on Port Beach Island; we were super-excited about life as it was unfolding. Our condo-on-the-beach had a huge balcony overlooking the ocean, and we spent hours drinking gin and tonics, bourbon and Cokes, and smoked one joint after the next. I remember snorting lines of cocaine—a wedding gift from one of his friends.

One night, somehow, we actually lost each other on the beach. We were both so "disoriented", neither could tell the other exactly what had happened. The day we left was no exception; I was inebriated to say the least. I jumped on the emotional roller coaster as I thought about school starting soon, and without me. I wasn't enrolled. My plans had changed so drastically, so quickly. Now I had none at all, well, basically. One call to Mom and Dad, and a check arrived the day after we got back to our tiny one-room apartment. We were preparing for whatever life would bring to teenaged newlyweds living in a college town.

Although I was legally an adult, my parents were still treating me like a child. Ok, so they were paying for school, but the fact remained they were disappointed in my quick change of plans to get married. It became obvious when they took Gretta away from me. They were *still* making the rules, and I had to adhere to the fact that since I was now "independent", or somewhat, I was on my own to find transportation.

"Let your *husband* buy you a car", they said. So, what the hell were *they* going to do with *my* car sitting in *their* driveway? Fuck it. I made due for a while, walking, riding the bus, catching a ride with Brad or a friend, whenever I needed one. I guess they got tired of my car in their driveway, because they eventually let me have it back. Sometimes it's better just to "throw in the towel".

I was waiting tables part-time at a popular bar-be-cue hangout, making good money and lots of friends. Every day meant another reason to party- grades, the weather, taking a breath- there was always some reason to drink, smoke dope and try whatever happened to be going around at the time. The day that marked our one-month matrimonial union was no exception. We had a party that Saturday afternoon and into the night at a nearby lake park, complete with kegs and margarita machines. People came all day long- old friends, new acquaintances; I do believe everyone had an absolute blast. Cheech and Chong would have been proud to say they were *our* friends; we were doing it up right. But as the night grew weary, so did I.

The crowd dwindled as guests staggered along to wherever it was they needed to be, wherever they would end up that night. I joined suit, finding my way to the car. As I opened my eyes, I remember us riding in our small sports car, Brad trying desperately to keep up with the van in front of us; it was housing the booze machines. Then, in an instant, it was as if we were riding on a roller coaster in the dark, with our eyes closed, and unfastened in the seat.

Oh my God! What's happening!?! The next moment I was laying on my side with blades of grass prickling at my nose. Where was the earth? Which way was the sky? The car was on its side—the passenger side, *my* side. The windshield was so close I could reach out and touch it, but I didn't dare. The glass now looked like a spider's web; it was cracked in a million shards. I heard distant voices.

"Get her out!! Hurry! The car's going to blow!" The voices grew closer and louder. All of a sudden, I felt hands grabbing me, pulling me upward, to my left, and through the driver's side window. Several people—I couldn't grasp what all was happening—were carrying me, frantically running away from the car. Then, BOOM!! I felt the Earth shake. Sparks were flying like firecrackers during a 4th of July celebration, and my body was immediately thrust downward. The people carrying me dove to the ground, or maybe were forced downward by the explosion.

Hours later, I was sitting in the emergency room getting bandaged up, doctors checking for broken bones and anything else that wasn't right. I was waiting for my in-laws to come pick me up. They had first gone to the jail to bond out Brad; he was being charged with a DWI. (He later got off on some lesser charge, thanks to his parents' money and their good lawyer). The officer had told them that as we and the oncoming car approached the same curve, we hit a patch of gravel. As Brad tried to overcorrect, we went tumbling three times, rolling over and over until landing on a cement embankment, on my side of the car. The passengers in the oncoming car had saved my life. I never got their names, nor had the chance to thank them. I was in a lot of pain, and very much shaken.

CHAPTER 12

THE SEMESTER WAS COMING TO an end, and I was seeing less and less of Brad. Seems he was always at the library, or so he said. We were arguing a lot, and not being around him was fine with me. As it were, I was spending time with my friends, usually at the pool or just hanging out at my apartment complex. I remembered the taste and feeling of daiquiris from long ago, so making a pitcher, or several, of daiquiris or margaritas had become part of my daily routine.

One particular day by the pool, I heard the sound of a motorcycle getting louder and louder as it approached the pool area. The rider stopped near me, and offered his "hello's" and a smile. *A really sexy smile.* He was easy on the eyes, and personable, too. Denny was about twenty years my senior, and married to a stewardess. She was always out of town, and he spent a lot of time at a friend's apartment—some guy who lived in my complex. Denny and I became friends, and spent a lot of time together over the next few months. After school, he'd pick me up and we'd ride all through the rolling hills and beautiful countryside. Smoking dope, snorting rails of cocaine and drinking whatever suited our fancy at the moment, was just part of our adventure. Denny never kissed me, but I wouldn't have minded it if he did. We had a great respect for each other, and were always just friendly. But we did had fun.

My birthday comes in the latter part of fall, when the Texas heat has usually cooled. The season boasts outdoor colors of rust, brown, gold and orange; I just love that time of year. This particular year Mom had planned a nice, quiet time for me to come home, the family gathering around and spending quality time together, and I was actually happy to have the sobering time away from Brad and the fast-paced, drug-induced world in which I was living. It was a nice weekend.

But when I walked in the tiny apartment I shared with my husband, I found it not only filled with the stink of smoke, but with about seven or eight other young men, friends of Brad. Some I knew—some more intimately than what Brad was privy to—and others I was about to meet, no doubt. Perry happened to be one of those guys.

Brad filled a glass with bourbon and cola, and brought it to me. I committed to joining in with the rest of them, although I was tired and actually not in the mood, especially after being fresh and sober for a few days. But, far be it from me to be a party pooper, and then it happened. Brad approached me with something I'd never seen before, a small colored piece of paper, almost the size of a speck.

"Here Marley, try this. It's some type of new speed." Though I had never seen "speed" that looked like that, I trusted Brad and took the speck. He knew me well and was well aware of the types of drugs I never wanted anything to do with. I did have my limits; it was about having fun, not self-inflicting a permanent brain-freeze.

Later that night some of the guys went home, but five of us crammed into the small two-door car of one of our buddies and took the scenic drive up "Devil's Revenge". It's a windy road through the hills and valleys of the countryside which is usually a 20-minute ride, if going the speed limit. We were going so slowly it took over an hour to reach the top of the hilly drive, because Spen, the driver, was freaking out, yelling for us to "SHUT UP!" His face was so close to the steering wheel I thought he was having vision problems. We were laughing so hard I swear someone had to have peed himself in that car. Donald and Rob were sporting these life-like masks that looked like Icky Twirp and Delphinium, or maybe it was Ajax, and making really funny jokes; we were laughing hysterically.

When we got to Devil's Revenge, we got out of the car and lay underneath an enormous oak tree in the full moonlight, and envisioned the tree's limbs as arms, reaching out to grab us. At one-point Donald grabbed a running armadillo by the tail as he scurried across the grassy knoll, and to this day I swear that could never happen again in five lifetimes—not to anyone! He didn't hurt the little fella, but that was the most spectacular thing!

After laughing ourselves into oblivion, we were famished. On the way back into town we stopped at a familiar all-night diner and stumbled or staggered in. We chose a large round booth at the back of the dining room, or perhaps the hostess chose it for us, knowing we were already being disruptive- in a good sort of way. The place was so bright with lights that when we looked into each other's eyes, we saw nothing but bowling ball sized pupils, which made the laughter increase, both in volume and duration.

Seven hours later, Brad and I lay atop our bedspread, unable to sleep. I recall my obiter dictum as I lay staring at the ceiling, "I think that was acid."

"I think you're right," Brad replied, nonchalantly. It was years later when thinking about that night, that I realized Brad knew exactly what he was handing his naïve, gullible wife. Asshole. He knew if *I knew* it was LSD, I never would have taken it. But, no permanent harm was done, and it actually opened up the doors to other times of "extreme" circumstantial good times. Risks I would *never* ask for or offer up, in hindsight.

CHAPTER 13

JEEZ. WE WERE DYING. OUR marriage, that is. Two very young, personable, outgoing people, living in the environment—a college town with a gazillion gorgeous, single people. The town full of nightclubs which consistently offered free drinks and free to get in; who the hell wanted to study? I was drinking like a guppy—not that it was anything new, but I was changing. We both were changing.

For the first time in our years together, Brad was getting physical with me, and not in a good way. We were always under the influence of one thing or another, and growing tired of each other, no doubt. My aggravation toward him had reached a record height.

One late afternoon after coming home from work—or wherever he'd been—I was cooking dinner like the good little wife I was pretending to be; still trying to be, really. He slammed a few cold ones and smoked a little doobie, when I proceeded to show him the "blue strip on the stick". I hadn't gone to the clinic to be sure, but I had a strong feeling I was pregnant. I had a smile on my face; I thought perhaps our thoughts had changed about the subject, howbeit I couldn't have been more wrong. He looked at me with mean, cruel eyes.

"I hope you can take care of it, and the two of you will be very happy. I certainly won't be around." *Seriously? What a jerk,* I thought. *What a fucking jerk!*

Detecting his drunkenness and anger, I decided to take my disappointment elsewhere.

"I'll be back in a while… I need some fresh air," and I headed for the door.

"The hell you will!" he hissed. At that moment, before I could reach the knob on the door, I felt myself being thrust ass first into the barstools and kitchen wall, his head in my stomach like a demolition ball.

As I gathered myself and what was left of that section of the room, I threatened to have him arrested if he as much as touched me once more. Since he had already had an unpleasant brush with the law a few months before, he in no way wanted to face the cops with an assault charge. Besides, he was an honor student, and the school would probably kick him out.

The stick wasn't "blue" after that incident.

~†~

Holidays were upon us once again, and we drifted slowly to Bridgeton to be with our families. He stayed with his; I with mine. We did, however, spend *some* holiday time together, but it was nice to get away—from each other.

Back at school and work, within a week I received a call from my agent. I had been asked to do a photo shoot in the thriving Metropolis area, where I'd pose for national poster and catalog ads for the new year. Bags packed, I said "Adios!" to Brad. School wasn't in session yet, and I'd be back just in time for registration. Plus, I could stop in and visit Mom and Dad.

When I arrived back to San Ramos—my little college town of no repent—students were coming back from holiday break, and everyone was ready to roll. And I'm not talking about study-wise. Parties were popping up all over town, as people everywhere were celebrating the New Year and new-found freedoms.

One night, Brad and I were getting ready to go our separate ways, probably to meet up later. Maybe so, maybe not. But we absolutely blew up at each other. Anger, frustration, jealousy—his emotions erupted like an active volcano spews lava. As I was finessing my coiffure, once again, he came charging at me like a linebacker after a quarterback. Inebriation had set in—for both of us—but this night was in some way different. He went his way and I went mine.

CHAPTER 14

THE NEXT MORNING BRAD WAS gone. He had planned on going to a bowl game with some friends, so I wasn't surprised, nor angry when I awoke and he wasn't there. But my hangover was, and it was the worse headache I have ever, ever experienced. Pain was throbbing in my head, all the way to my toes, and I could barely move my body, much less turn or lift my head.

I was scheduled to register for school that day; Mom had called to make sure I had everything I needed. She knew Brad had gone, and was "just checking" on me. I explained how horrible I was feeling. She asked if I had fever, and I told her I didn't think so, but that I had the worse headache ever—that it hurt to even breathe. I could hardly open my mouth to talk. She told me to go to the infirmary, and to call her when I returned from there, and registering. She knew something was wrong, that what I had was more than a bad hangover—she knew me well.

By mid-afternoon, I was in the same spot on the bed. The only movement I had made—besides my breathing—was to take aspirins and get up to get a trash can which I used as a disposal vomitorium. I was extremely lethargic, and lifeless.

A few hours later I awoke in the back of a Cadillac—my Grandmother's car. We were cruising down the highway at a high speed, and my two favorite ladies were in the front seat. It's amazing how mother's intuition takes precedence in situations where no one else knows what the hell is going on, not even the offspring.

"Stop the car!!" I mumbled. Grandmother pulled over, and I managed to open the door, hang my head out, and expel what was left in my pitiful body—bile and dry heaves.

~✝~

Over the course of the next week, I lay lifeless in my bedroom at my parents' home. I heard Mother argue with several persons on the phone, at different times of the day, for several days. Her frustration was spiraling, being put on hold and given appointments for me to be seen "in 4 days" at one clinic, and "3 weeks" at another.

"The emergency room doctors told us nothing about my daughter, except that she has a concussion. There's something much more serious going on, and I want her to have tests done," Mom demanded over and over. She waited for one doctor to call; called another and waited again.

"Marley is suffering from a concussion; she obviously has experienced a blow to the head—some type of traumatic experience. But she'll be fine and can go back home as soon as she feels well enough to do so," explained one neurosurgeon. The multitude of doctors I had been seen and tested by, concurred.

For ten days, I had been back in Bridgeton and lost 15 pounds. Everything that *tried* to go down my stomach, came back up. Mom had given me a few sponge baths, and had tried to brush my long locks, but to no avail. My head was hurting so badly I couldn't bear the touch of her gentle hands near my scalp. She and Daddy were frenzied with worry, but the only thing they could do was keep me at *their* home, and keep watching for my progress, or not. In no way were they about to let me go back "home", to my college town, to San Ramos. Not yet.

On the 13th day, I awoke feeling like someone who'd been sick, but not dead. *That* was an improvement. It was a beautiful, warming January day, and Mom thought it'd be a nice idea if we took a drive so I could get some sunshine and fresh air. So, we poured my weak body into something comfortable, and took a short drive, until I realized I was famished.

"Mom, let's go to that new seafood restaurant down the road. I'm so hungry, and some chowder sounds really good now. I think I can eat something." Although I was still quite ill, we were both glad I was up, and Mom was elated I had an appetite.

We had barely ordered the soup-of-the-day, when I exclaimed a howling "AAAAWWWWWHHHHHH!!"

In what seemed like slow motion, both of my hands went from my lap to my head, cupping the excruciating pain I was having as I felt my head was exploding. Had I been shot by a bullet? Was my brain bursting out of my head? The pain was unfucking believable!

The next thing I remember I was lying in a hospital bed with a nurse hovering over me asking me what day it was, what my name was, and whatever else. I was drifting in and out of consciousness; and would later find out I was nearing death. Very close to death.

6:12 p.m.: "Get her to surgery, NOW! She's got a blood clot on the brain! Cancel all my appointments!" The door burst open with a man in a white coat hurrying towards me with a collection of medical followers on his coattails.

The gurney was rushing down the hallway; all I could see were the lights overhead moving quickly. I vaguely remember images and voices on each side, like they were trying to keep up with me, and I was winning the race. One voice was talking in a Godlike manner, in a way only a priest could do; Mother was on the other side, responding, confessing my sins via proxy. *Wow…I didn't know she knew that…good things she does, I guess.* I was being given my Last Rites.

CHAPTER 15

MY EYES OPENED; NO EXCRUCIATING headache. Daddy was the first image in focus; he was looking at me as if I were a vision of excellence.

"She's the most beautiful thing I've ever seen", I heard him say, in a peaceful and pleasant voice.

His smile was so handsome, and his eyes were cloudy. A tear rolled down his cheek; his entire face was filled with love and relief.

"Hi, Daddy." I smiled, too.

Mom joined in on the other side of the bed. "Hello Sweetheart. How are you feeling?" She had saved my life.

The next week I was recuperating, resting, trying to gain any of the strength I had lost. The doctor—the only neurosurgeon who had read the test results correctly—had explained that the subdural hematoma putting pressure on my brain for two weeks had burst the day I was at lunch. I had barely lived through the next four hours, but wouldn't have made it through a fifth. It just doesn't happen, but miracles do.

Mom and Dad pondered the thoughts of medical malpractice, but they were very simple people, and grateful to have their baby girl alive and well. They didn't want us to be dragged through such chaos. We had been through enough.

~✝~

I couldn't look in the mirror; I didn't want to see myself. Ever since waking from surgery a few days ago and running my finger up, through the white turban encasing my head, I didn't want to look in the mirror. My long, beautiful hair was gone. It was now a souvenir, a memory, living in a large hat box. And it was still matted.

The days went by, and I was sporting a couple of real cool wigs, albeit in no way did they take the place of the real thing. I needed something to cover up my newfound baldness, no doubt, but also to cover the stitches and staples that connected the three holes drilled into my skull. The holes had to be drilled to drain the blood clotting, which was putting pressure on my brain.

With a couple of different wigs, one moment I could look like Pat Benatar with short, sassy hair. Then I could go in and come back out looking like Tina Turner, with a much wilder, carefree look. Ok, so it was kind of cool. But now it was time to do something about my problem—my *addiction* problem—or so the doctor said. You know—drugs, alcohol.

"He said it wouldn't have happened, Marley, if you hadn't been drinking. He said that alcohol causes your brain to shrink, and a blow to your head caused the clot to form between your skull and brain. He said people don't live through that. He said you shouldn't be here, Marley. We've got to get you some help, honey." I had to hear Mom tell me that, seems like a million times. I was wishing the doctor would shut the fuck up.

"He said! He said! He said! To hell with him! He doesn't know me, and he's not going to tell me what I need and don't need! Fuck him!" I was definitely not agreeing with what it seemed like everyone else was saying.

"But *we* know you, Marley. And we know there's a problem with drinking, and whatever else it is you do. Honey, we almost had to bury you. Please, please let us get you some help." Mom was making her point, and when she said the word "bury", she hit a nerve.

The semester was already in full force without me, and I was still in Bridgeton. I felt I was obligated to at least listen to the ones I love and who have suffered along with me, so, I agreed to *think* about doing *something.*

Over the years, I've often thought about that horrific night when it all started, and have tried desperately to remember what happened. What had I hit? Was it in the bathroom with Brad? Did he push me into the toilet, the bathtub? Did I fall down at one of the many parties I went to that night? Down the stairs, somewhere? I can honestly say, I don't remember. I spent much of that night in a blackout, and I'll never know. I have no idea what happened, that almost took my life.

Mother and Daddy didn't know where to look for this sort of help, or who to turn to. My medical bills were piling up, and I hadn't talked to Brad but two times in over six weeks. We didn't have insurance, and he didn't seem overly zealous about my physical and mental condition. I was in Bridgeton with my parents; guess he figured I was *their* problem. So, they sought and took the advice of a concerned physician.

CHAPTER 16

THE GROUNDS WERE LOVELY; TALL, majestic trees of oak and pecan hovering over thick, dark green carpets of St. Augustine grass. They seemed to be protecting it; probably been doing so for ages. Shaded, winding lanes leading to and from old but well-maintained red-brick buildings, perched within their fenced boundaries. As we drove in the entry way, I read the gate's words "State Hospital". Never in my life would I have imagined *I* might be living within these confines.

We must have had an appointment, because Daddy new exactly which building to drive up to. He parked the car, grabbed my small suitcase, and the three of us entered. He looked so sad; so different from what he had been expressing lately.

We went through some sort of security section, as if getting a clearance to enter the building. Definitely an institution, and one I was definitely *not* fond of. I remembered seeing places like this in old movies, and once the unlucky person went in, they were unlikely to come out. I wasn't liking the atmosphere, but I promised. I didn't know how long I was going to have to stay, nor what they would do to me.

The nurse assured us I'd be fine, howbeit I was having my doubts. With tears in her eyes, Mom hugged me. Then Daddy hugged me with as much uncertainty on his face as I had in my mind. As they left, the nurse showed me to my room; there were multiple beds and no one else in it. The moment I sat down, glad to be alone, she let me know I couldn't stay there "by yourself". *What the fuck?! No wonder no one else is in here!*

"You aren't allowed to be in any room, alone." She said, with the compassion of a fire-breathing dragon. "You must be in the day-room until it's evening, and the other ladies are here." Fine. Whatever. *So, take me to wherever the hell I'm supposed to be.*

But before introducing me to my fellow-patients, she went through all my belongings, and took half of the stuff out, and away.

"No perfume... no hairspray... and certainly no mouthwash." This lady was beginning to sound like a communist dictator instead of a nurse. *Aren't they supposed to be nice?* She told me that since they contained alcohol, I wasn't allowed to have them, *at all*. Before this moment, I had never thought about drinking my cologne. But me being here, she had a point.

Everywhere I looked, there were locked doors. Was I in prison, or just imprisoned in a fucking insane asylum; a bedlam of dolts? The few people who were in the "ward" seemed really strange. *Bless their hearts.* One man was sitting alone, practically motionless, making weird noises with his nose. At least that's what I thought, since his mouth never moved. A lady on the other side of the room was in a position not even a contortionist could mock. She looked like she was in pain, but at least wasn't making any weird noises.

Then there were the cardplayers sitting around an old wooden table, in a cloud of cigarette smoke. I almost gagged when I walked near them; one of them motioned to me to come over, so I strolled bravely toward the smoke cloud, and tried to make some "friends". The dictator had told me to "make yourself at home; make some friends", but I couldn't even go in my own room. And these people were weird. This wasn't seeming like any sort of "home" to me. *Oh my God, I see a phone!*

~✝~

Several hours had passed; *they'd be home by now.* I was wishing I was. I hated this place, and I was letting it get to me. I was scared. I picked up the phone and dialed.

"I hate it here, Mother! Please, please come get me!" I was crying, tearfully, my voice clearly shaken.

"Marley, you've got to give it a try. Just stay there through the night, and see what tomorrow brings, please." Mom begged me, and I could tell she was crying, too.

"It's not going to get any better! It's not! They're mean here, and everyone is so strange. I don't belong here. Please, Mom…please!" Tears were coming harder than before, and I was letting it be known.

Hours went by, and I kept calling, begging. Crying repeatedly, and showing it in my voice; in my words. Then anger crept in, with the fear.

Later that night—it seemed like forever had gone by—and I was sitting near the door I had once come through; the one that I knew was the way out. I saw them; Mom and Grandmother had come to rescue me from the perdition I had been forced to withstand, for hours. I was so happy to see familiar people. Grandfather was in the car. The three of them had come to take me home. But no…wait. They hadn't.

They had a plan, and I was the centerpiece. We were tired, and hungry. After a late-night dinner at a nearby diner, we drove to a motel—older but nice; no way in hell would my grandparents be caught dead in a dump—on the opposite side of town, but *not* the side closest to home.

After demanding to know why we were there and not on our way home, Mom explained to me that tomorrow we'd take a drive through the Hill Country, and just take a look at a place—a residential treatment center—that came highly recommended by a reliable resource. (Uncle Frank had stayed there and it seemed to have helped him with his alcohol problem). That's possibly the only other place my family knew anything about.

"Let's just look at it, and see if you like it; if you're comfortable. And if you aren't, we'll leave. I promise." She *promised*. Over and over I insisted, and over and over she promised.

The drive through the countryside was beautiful, and riding in the Cadillac felt like floating on a cloud. It was a beautiful, warm winter's day, and the water in the small river alongside the winding road seemed so calm and soothing.

"The Hills at the River Bend" actually looked like a mountain resort; it was lovely. Log cabins sat side by side overlooking a cliff-like edge, and bordering another side of the property was a lodge-like structure, sort of like a motel. Then the center boasted of a large swimming pool, which, of course, was empty for this time of year. And from the pool was a stone walkway which led to a large building; it reminded me of a clubhouse, or recreational area.

The lady we talked to was very cordial, quite reassuring. She took Mom and me for a tour of the grounds, and discussed various aspects of the program—its counseling and daily procedures. She showed us an art room, a model-cabin, and yes, the clubhouse. It was fine, but I wasn't about to *stay* there. I was ready to get back to *my* home, *my* life, *my* friends, and my husband, although we had hardly spoken over the weeks.

"Let's just sit down here, and allow me to get some information from you," assured the nice lady.

"*Remember…it's your decision, as to whether or not you want to stay, Marley…*" I had heard this over and over from not only Mom, but my grandparents as well. They were all waiting for me, out in the car.

As sure as I was telling the lady "thanks, but no thanks", I heard a car start, and a car door slam shut. I thought. I knew. I ran out the door and saw the big blue Cadillac driving off, without me. Mother was in the back seat, staring at me with sad eyes; I was running after her, after them. My suitcase was in the middle of the parking lot. I stopped, stood, and cried. *God damnit!*

The conniving bitch walked toward me. "They just want what's best for you, Marley. It's better this way." *What the fuck does she know?* I wanted to fucking hit her! *Well, it is a beautiful place*, I thought. And it sure beat the hell out of the snake pit I had been in the day before.

She called for some older guy to take my suitcase to my room. It was one of the motel-type rooms. *Hmm. Nice. A room with a view.* The bellman told me that if I need anything at all, to pick up the phone and call. I was actually impressed, but still pissed.

A pretty, young lady about my age walked in shortly thereafter, and said "Hi. I'm Anita. I'm your roommate, but I'll be leaving soon. I'm here for depression, and my husband and I are working out marriage problems. He comes here every weekend, and we're allowed to stay in the co-ed area (she pointed to another lodge-looking building, behind the rec-hall).” *Was she going to tell me when she was born, where she lived and when they had sex, too? Is it my time to talk now?*

"I'm Marley. And I'm here for…depression, too." Well, it was all depressing as far as I was concerned, so what the hell. She—nor anyone else—didn't need to know my problems. Besides, I didn't *have* a fucking problem with alcohol, or anything else for that matter. So, I like to drink, and had a bad experience (that I don't remember). My attitude was definitely lacking in congeniality.

Over the course of the next two weeks, roughly, I attended group session which I divulged only what I thought pertinent to anyone's knowledge. The art classes were interesting, and we dined in a beautiful spherical-shaped, formal dining room with glass walls along two entire sides, allowing the patrons a beautiful view of the countryside and flowing river below. Linen table cloths were changed daily, as were the floral arrangements on each table. The food was cafeteria-style, and some of the most wonderful food I had ever consumed.

But then, there were the AA meetings; the Alcoholics Anonymous meetings we were required to attend daily. And I wasn't about to admit I was an alcoholic. The other people there might be, but not me. No way; not until Jed, this one particular know-it-all kept on my ass about me needing to admit I was an alcoholic. He explained to me that an alcoholic is someone who drinks, and has problems resulting from it. Then she probably drinks again, and sometimes more. Jed the Jerk, I called him, and he was a nuisance to my sanity, but the things he told me and made me read, I couldn't deny. For the first time in my life, I said—in front of God and everybody— "I'm Marley…and I'm an alcoholic."

And then there was Dodie. He was a drummer in a band, and a heroin addict. He was adorable with big aqua-green eyes and beautiful sandy-blond hair—longer than my Pat Benatar wig. Dodie and I laughed constantly, and I fell in love. *We* fell in love, and had an affair.

Good sex, fun times laughing, and beautiful surroundings. Now *that* was treatment!

CHAPTER 17

CHECKING MYSELF OUT OF "THE Hills" was bittersweet; I wanted to stay in the beautiful scenic, tranquil resort setting with the man I was in love with, but I knew reality, and this wasn't it. Dodie and I saw each other a few times over the following months; I took a bus trip to West Texas to visit him, but this time, I did my partying *before* and *after* the bus ride. I wasn't about to be left out in the middle of the Texas desert by a pissed-off driver. We each returned to our respective spouses.

At the acid-party in my apartment a few months ago, I met one of Brad's friends, Perry. He was gorgeous; tall, dark and handsome, looked like an Indian. Excuse me—*Native American.* Gorgeous long, black, shiny hair, and about 6'3". Perry's voice was raspy, which meant *sexy* to me. He'd come over to see Brad, but I was sure it was *me* he was after, not Brad's friendship. Of course, I'd hang out with them at times, then just with Perry when Brad wasn't around, which was quite a bit. Perry and I began going out to friends' parties, or dancing at night clubs. We had a blast together, as we both adored music, laughter and dancing. Perry was very respectable about asking Brad if he minded we go out together, until the night he kissed me. Then kissed me again, and well, that led to an entire night of drinking, smoking dope and skinny-dipping. We both knew this had gone way beyond a platonic relationship. And we also both knew that my days married to Brad were numbered.

Because of my accident and recent stay in rehab, I wasn't enrolled in school but I was working. Perry was *supposed* to be enrolled—or so his parents thought—but he was spending their hard-earned money on us.

Concerts, drugs, drinking, road trips. Whatever we like to do to have fun, we were doing it. And we were in love—deep.

A friend of mine back home in Bridgeton was getting married that summer, and I was to attend the bridal shower a week prior. I couldn't make the wedding, so I was excited about the shower all the more, and to see Mom and Dad as well. So, I set out for a weekend of reuniting with high school friends and loved ones.

When the time came for me to mosey on back to my little Casa with the sometimes hubby, some of the girls decided to meet, eat and have some spirits before going our separate ways. Since I loathed eating and drinking at the same time, I usually chose to drink. No way could I get a good buzz going on a full stomach; that would limit my drinking. So, we met, they ate, I drank, and we left. I was looking forward to getting back to my college community and new-found love.

But, I was intercepted. By a cop and his damn flashing lights. I was fully loaded while cruising 93 miles an hour in a 70-mph zone. *Not good*. I really *was* in a hurry, and feeling absolutely lit. I spent half the night in jail, and was charged with a DUI. I didn't know where Brad was, and cell phones weren't around yet, so I called some friends from work, and they came to get me.

Never having been in trouble before, I was released on a Personal Recognizance bond, and went to my tiny apartment to try to figure out what the hell I was going to do with my life.

As much as I wanted to stay there with Perry, I knew I had to officially end it with Brad before going any further; we were fighting the little bit of time we'd spend together, and I was done with that shit. But I needed to be on familiar turf, with the people who could help me put my life back together.

Mom, Dad, Sissy and Bubba showed up at the apartment a week later, and proceeded to pack my things and move my belongings out of the apartment. I just stood there in a trance-like state as I reflected back on the year's events, and where I was going from here.

Not much was said while I rode with Daddy back to Bridgeton. "You've lived more in the past two years then I've lived in my entire forty-seven years of life,' he said, solemnly. I don't think I said a word.

~✝~

I enrolled in a private school part-time, taking administrative classes to brush up on my secretarial and administrative office skills, and secured a part-time job. Actually, I had *two* part-time jobs. One was through the school program, working for the city police department directly after class, and the other was waitressing at a popular new restaurant—evenings and weekends. It was a lot of fun.

But two days after filing for divorce, I walked, slowly into my lawyer's office. He looked at my face—eyes black and blue, swollen lip, fractured nose, scratches all over my arms and legs. "No more nightclubs. Lay low, and dress like you're going to Sunday school—every day," was his advice to me.

The previous night I had gone out; went to meet some friends and listen to a new band in town. Brad was there. I hesitated when he asked me to go outside and talk. "I just want to talk to you, Marley. We can't talk in here; it's too loud," he said, convincingly.

After stepping away from the door outside, he turned as if to tell me something, and with one blow to my jaw, I went straight down to the ground. He grabbed my arms, dragged me to the side of the building, and straddled my stomach, steadily beating and pounding my face and chest as if I were a boxer's punching bag. He got up and began to run off when he saw two of our friends come running, but they—two guys—grabbed him, and proceeded to give him the same pelting I had just received. Thank God for them; they had seen me go outside with Brad, and didn't like the way he was looking at me. What goes around, comes around.

CHAPTER 18

I WAS GOING THROUGH A divorce and Sissy was getting married; what household conversations we were having! The wedding was beautiful; the divorce was ugly. I was the bridesmaid, no longer the bride, but that was ok with me. Perry and I were still sort of an "item" but living 150 miles apart. That was ok, too. I was busy with work and school, and having fun partying with friends new and old, *every* chance I got. Back to my usual coming in all hours of the night.

I've heard tales that newlyweds are supposed to keep the top tier of their wedding cake in their freezer for the first year of marriage, and celebrate their anniversary by eating it. Well, Sissy and Doug never got a chance to do that with theirs. I ate it—over the course of a the few months I lived with Mom and Dad.

Mom promised Sissy she'd keep the lovely cake for her and Doug, and have them over for their first anniversary celebration. But when the day came to celebrate the jolly time, there was no cake. With all the nights I came in drunk and stoned, having the munchies, well, I have to say that cake was absolutely scrumptious! Little by little I tried to have control, but to no avail. It was delicious! Magnifico! I never meant to do any harm; it just happened, and I have *never* since gotten such a vocal lashing that I did that day when Sissy found out. But, Mom ordered a new cake, and they celebrated, anyway. All was good, or, ok.

My courses in school were finished and I was now a Certified Administrative Aide—with a 4.0 average. Not bad for a party girl; one who had gone through so much shit, already. I landed a job with a prominent, local businessman and less than one month into my job, he asked me to go with him on an all-expense paid trip to Mexico—just for fun, not business. I obliged his wishes and flew for the first time, scuba-dived—first time as well—the Caribbean and had an affair with my boss, all in the same week. We were both single, and Perry was seeing other girls, anyway. Boss Man was a big-time drinker, smoker, and line snorter—a guy after my own heart, and wealthy, too. Made for an even better time! We had parties together, traveled for a while, and he even asked me to quit my job.

"Marry me and let me support you, forever. You're beautiful, and I love you", he kept proposing, I remember once in Bermuda when we were drinking; he kept trying to get me to go to bed with him, and I pretended to be passed out. I wanted the trinkets and the fun, but I wasn't in love, and definitely not ready for *that* trip—down the aisle. I turned down offers of cars, boats and a fine bank account; I knew nothing good comes free, and I wasn't ready to pay that price. Nevertheless, we continued—for a while—to spend a great deal of time together having fun.

~†~

My divorce from Brad was final, and I was free. We had made amends; we were both made of good character to be enemies. He and I would always care for one another, our lives had taken different paths. That happens when you're still growing.

I'd made a new and dear-to-me friend while working for my previous boss; her name was Stacee, and she was a hoot! Wonderful kid, but a bedlamite at best—much like me. We were both blond, outspoken, and absolutely adored a good time. The more we got to know each other, the more we realized our vast circle of friends were some of the same. *What a small world.*

Often, we'd close the bars down in Bridgeton, and after deciding we weren't through partying, get in the car and cruise to one of the nearest metroplexes—where the clubs stayed open later, and friends never slept.

One week in particular, we decided to take a road trip to my old stomping grounds, San Ramos. We both had many friends between here and there, and just *knew* it would be nothing but fun, fun, fun. We were *dead* wrong.

Stacee had a particular pair of friends she wanted to visit in Austin. Any friend of hers are friends of mine—that's how we rolled. Since she was doing the driving, I was taking every advantage of it—drinking, smoking, the usual.

We'd been "visiting" with these folks for a while; I'm not sure how long. I was pretty lit. Apparently, I needed something out of the car, because I went down to the parking lot where we were parked. Because it was a Friday night and the complex was crowded with vehicles, we had to park in a lot across the street from the particular unit we were visiting. I never made it back up to that apartment.

The next thing I remember was that I was riding in the back seat of a car; a car load of Mexicans I didn't know. There were probably seven or eight of us in the car, at least; all men except for me, and one other woman. She was in the front. *I have no fucking idea who these people were!* They were smoking reefer and laughing, and I had been kidnapped. Taken.

I begged them to let me go, to let me out. I didn't care where we were; I just wanted to get out of that car. I was scared, real scared. At one point the car pulled over near an overpass. I wasn't quite sure where, but knew it was on the outskirts of town. I could see the halo of lights far off in the distance. A couple of the guys got out of the car, and pulled me out with them.

"Come on baby, let's dance", one said as he was swaying. He was more drunk and stoned than anything else. But he wasn't talking about dancing. As he turned me around—my back facing him—he tried to bend me over. I had on a dress, and I was sure he was going to rape me.

"Please, please do whatever you want with my body, but kill me first." I specifically remember telling him those exact words. Pleading.

All I could think about was my parents. I was going to be raped, or even die out here, and they'd never know. But it didn't happen that way.

The guy laughed and just shook his head. We all got back in the car, and drove away.

As I was sandwiched in the front seat now, the driver leaned over to me, promising, "You'll be ok; I'll take you wherever you want to go after I drop them off. Nobody wants to hurt you; they're just having fun."

We made several drop-off points, until there were only the two of us left in the car. Then he started groping, grabbing for me; pulling me toward him as he was driving, swerving on country road. *Oh, dear God, no!*

"What are you doing?! I thought you were going to help me!" I screamed. Now I was really scared; alone with this guy, far away from anywhere I knew. But I saw lights. They were coming from a distance; from what looked like a gatehouse, or guard house. It was now about to be dawn; I could see skylight on the verge of existence. Neither of us knew where we were; the vast openness wasn't familiar.

"Ok, I'll do whatever you want, but let's go over there and find out where we are first," I was persistent, and convincing. I was pointing to the guard house.

As we drove toward the small dwelling, I could tell the interior it protected was something military, but I had no idea what. What I did know what that someone was in there, and that's all that mattered. We stopped, and as the guard approached the driver side of the car—my stupid-ass driver actually getting ready to ask him directions to somewhere—I let out a blood-curdling scream as I bolted out of the car, running around it, and into the small shack.

"Help me! I've been kidnapped! Help me, PLEASE!" I was giving my lungs a workout, and I hit the floor as soon as I got inside. I was truly freaked out.

The next moments happened so fast. I remember the guard pulling a gun on the driver, and calling the cops. They were there, immediately.

After asking me if I was going to press charges and making sure I was all right, they took the guy in for something to do with drugs—possession, whatever. I never wanted to see this guy again. And if I did press charges, what sort of statement would I make? I don't remember a large part of the night—how I got in, or was forced in the car. So many particulars were gone, lost. Blacked out of my memory. I just wanted to get out of there and be some place safe, familiar.

The Average Joe—or in my case, Jane—didn't carry cell phones. I didn't know anyone around that area I could call at that time of morning whom I knew would help me; then I thought of Brad. He would do anything for me, *wouldn't he?* I called him; and he was on his way. *I never was so glad to see anyone in my life!* He took me to his apartment, where I spent the remainder of the day, the night, and the next day.

I finally got in touch with Stacee, as she was frantic with worry. She'd been up for two days straight, calling everyone we knew, even the police—to let them know she was worried, and would soon be filling a missing person's report. She hadn't called my parents, and was horrified she'd have to do so. Of all the people I didn't want to find out where I was that weekend, Brad was the *one* I needed, and turned out to be my hero.

CHAPTER 19

VERY FEW PEOPLE EVER HEARD about that night; certainly, Perry didn't. I didn't want to create chaos with *our* relationship, especially since Brad had come to my rescue and I'd spent time at his place recuperating and, well, Perry was dealing with his own issues.

Back in Bridgeton, I was trying to settle down a little by living a pretty basic life—work, pay bills, have some fun, but *stay out of trouble.* Perry and I were spending more time together, really being in love. We had become inseparable, but for the miles between us. I didn't realize the extent of Perry's lying; of course, he *would never* lie to me, and other people were all just, crazy.

His parents had cut him off financially—they'd found out about his lying about being in school. *How could they be so cruel?* He was such a great guy, so I thought. He could do no wrong in my eyes, but my eyes were blurred. In fact, I was totally blinded by love—totally.

But he moved in with me, and we did all right for a while. We both worked, and we both partied. The usual—mainly drinking and smoking dope, pot. It was our way of life; a daily way of life. We were having fun—going out dancing, traveling to concerts, whatever we wanted was at our fingertips.

We became friendly with a couple; Perry worked with the guy, and his wife seemed like a nice person. Now and then we'd socialize at their house, sometimes our apartment, a bar or dancehall. But when holidays rolled around and she told us she wanted to give *me* to *her husband* for

Christmas, oh, and *watch,* well, we never hung out with them again. That wasn't our style, and that was just weird. *Never a dull moment!*

My becoming pregnant was a huge game-changer for us. Although it was unplanned, Perry was elated. I was happy, but he was overwhelmed with joy. He immediately wanted to be married, but I'd already been up and down that road recently, and wasn't about to go there again. Howbeit, Mom was on his side. She decided that if we were going to have a baby, we'd do it the moral, old-fashioned way. I didn't feel good about rushing into another marriage, and told them both that if all went well in the next months, I would be happy to say "I do".

But, with two against one, their persistence won out, and Perry and I waltzed into a local JP's home one night—Mom and Dad in-tow—and exchanged our vows. We had a small reception at the house afterward, and although no big deal, it was sweet. Perry was truly happy, and as much as I loved him, seeing his sexy smile and joyful heart helped to sway my vote about our present situation, and near future.

"Oh shit! Mother!!!" I was bleeding profusely from between my legs, and having horrific stabbing-like pains in my stomach area. Two days into the marriage and I was having a miscarriage. Perry had dropped me off to spend the afternoon at Mom's while he worked, and I had taken a few days off to rest. The pain was overwhelming, and I was losing so much blood. We got to the doctor's office right away, as I was definitely told I'd lost the baby. Perry was in shock; he remained aphonic for a few days after. And although I was disappointed, I knew in my heart something was wrong. And honestly, with all the drinking and smoking I'd done up to finding out I *was* pregnant, I saw it as God's blessing. But it changed Perry; he was truly effected.

For a while we strived on—working, doing the things young married couples do. But our fun, loving relationship was never the same after the miscarriage. Weird shit was happening; more so than usual. Checks were bouncing to the point that I had to go to the bank more than once to clear up a "misinformed teller". Or I balled out the utilities rep because our electricity was shut off. *What the fuck is going on? Everybody's an idiot and no one can explain anything!*

But then, it happened. I opened a drawer in Perry's office one day while waiting for him to get back from lunch. I had stopped by to let him know *another* company was calling for collection, and I needed to know what to do. *This was all fucking insane!*

The bills—months' worth of bills—were piled in the drawer. Nothing had been paid in a very, long, time. He'd been writing hot checks to who knows where, and not paying the bills with the weekly paychecks I'd handed him to take to the bank. He had lied, and I'd caught him—red-handed. But because *both* of our names were on all accounts, I was in just as much trouble.

I'd ended up paying excessive fines to every place we had dealings with; even the sheriff's office got involved. I had to pay hot check writer's fees to cover all the damage that'd been done so neither of us would end up in jail, and it took quite a while. I finally was able to sign a sworn affidavit stating Perry had acted solely in these events, in case anyone or business was to pursue legal action in the future. Although an embarrassing, even humiliating occurrence, I got us through the difficult times and took over the household budgeting and management. Perry had spent money on drugs, going out with friends, and as far as I knew, other women. People had warned me; situations had warned me, but I didn't listen. I was love-struck, and living in a world of dolts. My Perry had been infallible, and in hindsight, I was the biggest, most naïve idiot of all.

We were arguing constantly by now, and hating each other as much as we loved. One night I asked him to leave—just for a while. We were fighting, and one of us needed to leave the premises. I needed to be away from him. But he wouldn't go, so I did.

I drove to a friend's house, but she wasn't there. So, I drove to another's—still, no one home. I drove to the bar where I used to frequent, and I would know some of the people there. After drinking a little, dancing a lot, it came time for me to go. As much as I didn't want to face Perry, I was hoping he'd be asleep by the time I got home. But I didn't make it home that night.

We lived in a suburb of town, and knowing I'd been drinking, although I wasn't drunk, I thought I'd play it safe and take the roads less-traveled to our apartment. As I came to a rolling stop at a 4-way intersection in BFE, the car coming opposite my direction was about to pass me. It didn't; the cop car's red lights went on, then the blue, and it turned around immediately. I was busted because of the rolling stop, five miles from anywhere. DWI #2. I went to jail, bonded out, and ended up doing two years' probation, successfully. *Damn!*

Broken in every way, I agreed to a stint in rehab at the pleading of my parents, and Perry. There was nothing left to lose, and I needed to sober up. At least if Perry wasn't going to help himself, maybe if he saw *I* was getting help for not only myself, but him as well, he'd shape up. We needed to get straight, and I was ready to do so.

After 28-days in a successful rehab program for drug and alcohol addiction—I suppose depression was thrown in there as well—I walked out of St. Vince's feeling revigorated and refreshed, wonderful and healthy—mind, body and soul. Perry had come to see me, but had moved back in with his parents near Houston at their insistence. He told me *they* were helping *him* get therapy, and we were talking quite frequently on the phone. I was sober, and loving it. But still, something wasn't right.

Three months later—still sober—I spoke with Perry the day before our first anniversary. We talked about the endless possibilities of our reconciliation, and of getting together the coming weekend to do something special, to celebrate our anniversary and our future.

"I'll call you tomorrow and we'll make plans. I love you, Marley."

"Can't wait. I love you, too, Perry."

Tomorrow never came.

As the days and weeks went by, devastation set in deeper and deeper. The call never came. I never heard from Perry again. Never. I tried to call his parents, but the number was disconnected. I had no idea where he'd gone, and never found him. He had disappeared from the earth, and took his family with him. I guess what he had told me months before about his parents possibly going overseas and working as missionaries was true; but did he go, too? Had they just packed up and left, without telling me anything? Was it all a lie? Perry was a psychopathic, habitual liar, but how did our lives get to this? Now I was just a damned fool; a very sad, depressed fool.

I remember one-day Grandmother came over to comfort me. Mom had asked her to, because I was so depressed I didn't get out of bed for days. Nobody could help me, not even my own Mom. I had missed work, and life. Grandmother sat down next to me as I lay in an ocean of tears, and she just talked, gently consoling me. I made the decision then and there that no matter whatever happened in my life, I would never again allow myself to get so lost in a man—a human being—that I lose myself.

CHAPTER 20

EARLY IN THE NEW YEAR, as far as I knew, I was still legally married. Months had gone by since I'd spoken with Perry, but I still jumped when I heard the phone ring. I didn't run to the mailbox anymore, but usually walked quickly. But, I was now working as a fitness trainer at a popular gym; aerobics was all the rage, and I was an instructor as well. Thank God for physical activity and good health, because it was helping me get through these times emotionally and mentally.

As much as I hate to brag, I have to say that I was in awesome shape; I guess I looked as good as I felt. We—the instructors—were all ladies in our twenties, and not bad to look at. And as evenings were slow at the gym, it was to definitely to our advantage. We'd spend time primping and prepping for going out dancing and drinking; changing into divas of the nightlife.

But no primping party was complete without the usual bottle of bourbon, a couple of joints and a line or two of our favorite white powder. Sometimes one of the managers would have to get an after-hours plumber to come unstop the toilet—often she tried to flush syringes and they'd get stuck halfway through the pipes. But to each their own; that just never was my thing.

Abigail—Gail for short—and I were practically sisters, in a way. Both tall, lanky, long wild hair—her mane was brunette, mine blond— and outgoing personalities to say the least. Did I mention *gorgeous?!* Ok, so I'm tidbit braggadocios. *It's my story…I can do that.* Two lionesses set out to prey on the hunks of the less-fortunate gender. Well, to be able to keep company with one or both of us, I guess I'd say they were the *luckier* gender—but only in that aspect.

Clubs came alive when we walked in. Our presence meant "let's get this party started!" Everyone knew that. We were queens of the dance floor and certainly every man's wish, and every woman's envy. We toasted the nights away and all that's within.

Gail and I had some really great friends of the local hairband era. She ended up marrying one bandmembers and I befriended another in various ways. *We remain close to this day.*

One night in particular, I'll never forget. Gail and I offered to take a friend to the airport, but one which was over 100 miles away, in the vast Metropolis area. Naturally, a road trip consisted of smoking pot, listening to hard rock and enjoying our style of refreshing beverage(s). Since I wasn't driving, I definitely took advantage of enjoying the back-seat freedom while the other two piloted us to the big city.

After dropping our friend off at the airport, Gail and I decided to indulge in the city lights and bless the party-patrons with our presence. So, we drove over to the downtown area where the streets were alive with restaurants, nightclubs, and dance halls of all sorts. We were free to be us, which meant dancing in the street, bar-hop, and laugh with every passer-by with whom we engaged. We were dressed to kill and we owned the world that night.

At one point, I saw a white, stretch-limo double-parked in front of two particular clubs where we had been "entertained". I—being in-quisitive in nature, especially when under the influence—was inclined to "inquire within". As I opened the back door and peered in, I was immediately eye-to-eye with a gorgeous Blair Underwood look-alike chauffeur. There was an instantaneous bond as we smiled at each other. I turned to Gail, grabbed her arm and pushed her into the backseat of the limo. With me on her heels, I closed the door, and off we went into whatever wild late-night yonder our laughing asses took us; or I should say wherever the *driver* was headed. Didn't know; didn't care. We were having the time of our lives!

After about an hour of driving around the brightly-lit city lights and finishing off the champagne obviously *not* meant for us, we ended up back at our starting point. No one hurt, nothing gained but some laughter and another spontaneous adventure. Gail and I thanked "Blair", got out, and went on our way to venture further into the night's surprises.

After hours of dancing, laughing and walking street after street—Downtown in the Metropolis boasts of a vast and most popular night life area in our Lone Star State—I just had to remove my heels and plot right down on the sidewalk I was standing. My feet were beat, as were my legs and lungs (from laughing so much, that's all). A free spot—free from parked cars and limousines—on the curb was sending me an invitation to rest, and my RSVP was returned immediately.

People-watching was also a favorite hobby of mine throughout my life, and tonight was no exception. With my feet free of shoes, and a curb that was by now as comfortable as a cushioned couch-seat, I rested my weary bones, breathed in the night's fresh air and watched as people all around me carried on; some in their romantic aura, others in their drunken stoopers. Or, some a bit of both. Then there was a guy. He apparently had the same idea I'd had; to rest and people-watch, that is. Or, possibly he liked what he saw and decided to join me in my leisure. *I'm sure the latter was his deciding factor.*

Ray was hilarious! He kept me laughing hysterically at silly things he was saying about passersby, and we made an instant, friendly connection that I'd rarely found with anyone else. He was obviously very outgoing; we had that in common, and we sat and talked for what seemed like hours. We actually ended up having decent, adult conversation. *Fancy that!*

His voice was low and soft—sort of with a wispy sound, and his smile was very sweet. He even looked a bit like "Rocky"; with a crooked smile. So, I dubbed him "Rocky Ray", or "Double-R" for short.

We found that we'd both been married and divorced more than once, and at such a young age. We like to smoke pot, drink, dance and laugh. Our families even had a few things in common. *What are the odds?* We both made a new friend that night.

~✝~

During the coming weeks, I traveled back and forth to spend time on the weekends with Ray and is friends. I even met his parents one evening; they were real nice people—*most* of them. He was calling me quite frequently, and even offered to come and get me a couple of times when my car was in the shop. He and a buddy would drive to Bridgeton, visit with Mom and Dad for a while, ensuring them I was safe in their presence and would be looked after as such. Ensured them they'd bring me back in one healthy piece, as well. So, off we went, the three of us on more weekend adventures in the big city of revelry, interesting people, and our favorites—drugs and alcohol.

One of our very first dates, however, probably should have been our last. Of course, we were loaded with one thing then another, and he got pulled over for something stupid coming back from a barbecue dinner at a country restaurant. We had taken the scenic route. Ray mouthed off, was arrested and charged with a DWI. But as I sat in the next cell (now I had gotten a Public Intoxication since the cop wouldn't let me drive), I laughed harder than I had in months, due to Ray's climbing the bars like a monkey, somehow pulling the Sheriff's radio close to his own cell so he could change the station, and just being a pure nut. The officers laughed as they shook their heads, and ended up letting us go so they wouldn't have to put up with more of Ray's "stunts".

But, Rocky Ray and I actually were becoming pretty good friends. Sure, we were now a dating item, but we were friends more than that. We just had so much fun together, and most importantly, Double-R was making me laugh. He was helping me get past the Perry thing, which was still very difficult.

After a particular discussion we had regarding the time we were now spending together, and trekking back and forth on the highway, he offered to let me live with him for a while if I wanted to move to the big city. There were more opportunities for me there, and I could make a fresh start, he reminded me. He was very sensitive when talking about my situation; Ray had compassion, and a caring heart. He would stop the car, get out and hold up traffic if it meant helping a senior citizen cross the street. So, it was decided. I transferred my aerobic-instructing job to a health-club in the Metropolis, packed up and moved in with Rocky Ray.

Even after a few months setting up house, he reminded me that a year had gone by since I had last heard from Perry.

"Don't you think it's time to end it, Marley?" he asked me one afternoon. "You need to get the divorce finalized, and move on with your life." He was right; he even escorted me to my hometown courthouse to get the divorce-ball rolling, once and for all. And so, it was done, as well. Ray held me on the steps of the courthouse that day, as I wept.

But all wasn't so peaches and cream with Ray, as it had started out to be. There were things I found out about him as our time together progressed; things I'd want to watch my own back for; things which were beginning to scare the shit out of me.

I found out through some of his closest friends that he had very jealous tendencies—something I hadn't seen in him until this point, since we were mainly friends. But as time passed, he was becoming more possessive with my time and attention, and I would soon learn of his maniacal outbursts. Before me, Ray went into a jealous rage over a recent girlfriend. He admitted that the result of his anger was the death—accidental as it were, but death, still—of the *other guy*. I was beginning to fear not for myself so much, but for any man who might look my way, say something sexist, complimentary or offensive—to Ray or me, either one, or just catch him at an unpleasant moment. And he was beginning to make ominous remarks about the way I dressed, which was one of the things that attracted him to me in the beginning of our "charade". Ray's true colors were coming out, and they weren't pretty.

CHAPTER 21

ROCKY RAY'S CONTRACT JOB HAD come to an end, and I was working temporary office jobs to make more money; the health club I'd worked at closed down, and we were having to make employment changes.

We'd moved into a newer apartment on the north side, but the only furniture we had was a mattress, two lawn chairs and a television with a screen the size of my palm. Oh, and I had clothes; lots of clothes.

Money was scarce, and after the bills were paid, there was little to live on—food, alcohol and weed cost money. So being the free-spirited, music-loving, fashion-chic that I was, I realized I could make good money—fast money—doing the things I loved doing. Dress up, dance to some great music, make fantastic money, oh, and did I mention be the center of attention? *That* was

Of course, considering Ray's jealous temper, we had a discussion about my potential future career, but also knowing how he loved partying and the money it took to do so, he was all in when the decision was made. Off to the dance club I went. Very upscale and classy, the placed I danced was for the elitist of gentlemen, and for the short time I did so, we were able to buy some much-needed furniture, pay off some bills, and even get ahead a little. Actually, I found out I could do occasional amateur nights, make out like a bandit, and keep my temporary day jobs. *It was a win/win for everyone!* Those days were short-lived, as well.

Ray was becoming increasingly abusive. The more time we spent together, the more possessive he became. Although we were never in love, he told me later he'd always considered me a *challenge*. I never knew if he meant the challenge of our personalities against each other, or the challenge of keeping me as "his", and being able to maintain a monogamous relationship with each other.

I do know he was very jealous when I'd dress immodestly at times, especially if he'd been under the influence. There were times he threatened to blow up my entire closet of clothes by igniting a lighter while spraying an entire row of clothes with hairspray. Slightly torching my clothes is what he was doing. How he didn't burn all of them *and* our apartment down is beyond me. I've often wondered how the hell I got into these messes, and how I ever got out.

One time I came home from being out with friends. Ray and I'd had an argument, and I went to the afternoon matinee with some of my best girlfriends. I walked in my bedroom to find a gas can sitting on the dresser, with wires hooked up and attached to dresser drawers and closet door knobs. The microwave in the kitchen looked like it had been disassembled. There was a book laid out on the table which read How to Make a Bomb with Household Items.

"Ray! Get in here and get this shit off my stuff and out of my room!" I was furious. Without rebellion or retaliation, he did.

"I just don't want you to leave me," was his only response. "I'm sorry." Now, the thoughts were definitely scurrying through my mind.

He had punched me in the stomach for dancing in the kitchen to a new album I'd bought; he didn't like the fact that the living room drapes were open in mid-afternoon. Then there was the time he gave me a fat lip for talking to some guy at the supermarket. The guy had asked me if I liked a particular item he'd seen in my basket.

I wanted to leave him, but it wasn't that easy. He must have been reading my mind when he told me if I left him my body parts would end up in "several dumpsters", along with threats of hurting my family and pets. I stayed out of fear not just for myself, but for those I loved. I would take the abuse if it meant my loved ones were safe. Ray was drinking more and more, and because of the situation, so was I. I didn't want to think, or feel. I just wanted to be…wasted.

But the final straw for me came when he took me out into a wooded area to kill me. *Fuck it; I'm going to die one way or another, and I'll be damned if I'm going to let him decide how it will be.* At least I needed to *try* get out of this tumultuous relationship.

That horrible day, we had been running errands for whatever reason, and he knew I was making an escape plan. The time had come, and he just knew. We hadn't been talking much as of late, and we were both very quiet that day.

Instead of turning down the busy street toward our apartment, he turned down an isolated road leading to the secluded woods near our complex.

"Where are we going? Why aren't you driving back to the apartment?" I asked. The day was a dreary, gloomy winter's day. No cheerful sunshine; no flowers along the roadside. Just a gray, foggy day. Depressing.

"I want to go talk where we won't be interrupted," he replied, not ugly or rude, but calm-like. The calm before the storm, I realized later. I wasn't excited about the coming journey, but I wasn't in the driver's seat, either.

The car stopped, and he looked over at me, with a tear falling down his cheek. "I'm going to kill you, then myself," he said. His voice was very soft, very sad. Very serious.

He explained to me that he couldn't let me leave him, although he admitted he wasn't in love with me. There was love, in a way; more like a connection, a bond. He'd told me he'd never met anyone like me, and he admired me tremendously. He was miserable, and we were *both* going to die for it.

"I'm confused," he said. "I don't want you like I want a wife, but I don't want anyone else to have you, either. I'm very confused." As much intelligence as I knew this guy had, he was fighting his own mind's mental and emotional chaos. There were demons within, and I had to find a way to help him, if I was going to help myself.

We were out of the car. I was trying to sway him any way I could. *If only I could run; run down the muddy road and find help.*

As I looked down the road, trying desperately to figure out what my next move would be, Ray picked up a rock—a large rock.

"If you try to run, I'll throw this rock and hit you in the back of the head. You know I will." I knew he would. "And then I'll kill myself. I have a gun in the car."

"Ray, listen, we need to get home. Let's go home, please. We can talk there, ok? Let's go to the liquor store on the way home, and pick up stuff to drink." I'm sure I specified what "stuff", but not sure after all these years. 'Please, Ray. Let's go get some booze, and go home. I promise we will work this out. You don't want to do this. I know you don't want to do this."

With tears in his sad eyes and fear in mine, we *did* go to the liquor store. That was the only time in my life I believe alcohol ever did me a favor. Suggesting we "drink" saved my life. *But I certainly don't suggest it on any regular, life-terms.* If we hadn't been fucked up from the booze in the first place, this relationship nor incident would never have happened.

Very soon after that day, I called the cops on Ray. I knew he possessed a few illegal weapons—knives, switchblades from Mexico—and I took that opportunity to turn him in. For all I knew he would use them on me, anyway. I needed time to get out, and this enabled me to do so. They took him away, and as he spent the night in jail, I had my closest friends help me move. Fast, and furiously, they helped me get out. I told the cops about his threats to my family, and as quietly as I could, let them know to be careful in their comings and goings. I had rented an apartment, paying for the entire month, not knowing exactly what day I'd be moving in. But I had the key, and the apartment was mine—alone, without Ray. A new beginning, and I was

Life was good, once again, and I was on top of the world. Living in my tiny, brand new apartment, I had all the friends a girl could possibly

want. Mostly because my dearest friends were also people I worked with; my new job as a corporate secretary. Making good money, and a respectable position in the community, I was totally independent and loving every minute of it!

Rocky Ray actually admitted his wrongs, and we remained cordial for a while. It was when my precious apartment was broken in to, that I realized who was to blame. Who else would have ransacked my closet, but Ray? I knew it was him, and a couple of my new "friends" made sure he understood what loyalty really meant, when they phoned him, threatened that he'd end up "in several dumpsters", and threatened his family and pets as well. Never, never again, did Ray bother me. Never. I think I actually got *another* apology out of him.

CHAPTER 22

"HI!" I THREW OUT THE words with a smile that matched my beautiful 3-piece pink and lavender pantsuit and with my most southern accent. I sat on the barstool inside the Mexican restaurant, along the highway. He was absolutely gorgeous; the bartender, reciprocating the enthusiastic look he was being tossed. When his gaze met mine, I knew this was the beginning of something special—*very* special. I would later hear him say that for him, it was love at first sight. He had never seen anyone so beautiful, so confident, and so intriguing. He told me that on that particular day, I seemed to be very happy. For me, I didn't know if it was love, or lust, but I was willing—and wanting—to find out.

Thursday evening, and I was just beginning my 10-day Florida vacation. I was in a great mood, and seeing this handsome face got my holiday off to a terrific start. Happy hour just got happier, as I was headed to Bridgeton to stay a night with Mom and Dad, but stopping for a couple of glasses of vino before heading out of town.

Miguel was the quintessence of the Italian male; he was a beau ideal. Tall with a prize-winning physique that screamed "hurt me so good", and thick dark hair wisping over deep, brown handsome eyes. I was ready to spend every moment of my vacation with him, but plans were made and I had an agenda—a *vacation* agenda, at least for now. I'd be back; I knew I would.

We talked, smiled, and talked some more. I certainly wanted to get to know Miguel better—much better—but for now I had to scoot. Miguel kindly offered to escort me to my car, and I obliged, accordingly.

I'd just purchased a new car, and a fine sports car at that. The license plate read "PRINC-S", but at this moment, I was feeling like a queen. Miguel handed me his phone number as he opened the car door for me, and requested I call him the moment I got back in town. *That's a move I was already planning on making.*

~†~

Florida was fun and restful. Since I was with Mother, I was on my best behavior. Just a few cocktails with dinner now and then, and of course some questionable looks from Mom. But nothing drastic happened, and it was a nice trip. We sightsaw, experienced a bit of history over the miles, and didn't argue *too much* on the way back.

I remember the day Lucy Ball died; that was sad news. Mom and I were headed to Disney World, and Sissy called to see how things were going, and asked if I wanted to go with her to the Bahamas in a couple of weeks. She told me she'd come across a deal we just couldn't pass up, so I said "of course", and told her we'd talk when I got back to Texas.

Rushing to get back to Miguel, I damn near pushed Mom out of the car when I came through Bridgeton, and headed back to the thriving Metropolis. I couldn't have gotten back faster unless I was magic and twitched my bewitching nose.

The moment I came within the city limits, I called Miguel to let him know I was back in town, and when he spoke the words, "…come to me", I about had an orgasm. But—deciding to make that wait—I jumped in my little hot-rod and headed to his casa.

There we were with the smiles again. He was gorgeous, and he thought the same of me. Two sexy peas in the same libidinous pod. Pot-smoking lovers immediately; things were heating up fast.

Miguel and I spent the next six months together almost constantly. We were either spending time at my apartment pool, or riding through the countryside on his motorcycle. Every time I heard the bike—sometimes miles away—my heart skipped beats, and I anticipated full-throttle excitement. We were rarely seen without a drink in one hand and a joint or bong in the other, and we liked things that way. And, since he worked nights and me days, he ended up staying with me so we could be together as much as possible. We were literally living together.

I went to the Bahamas with Sissy, and we had a good time. Well, except for the arguments we had about me drinking too much. One night I went out dancing in the clubs at the hotel; Sissy wanted to stay in, and do whatever she wanted to do. I ended up getting a black eye with a knot on my head. Not sure how that happened, except that perhaps it was caused from the punk music and head-banging on the dance floor. That's the only thing I could think of. There were no fights, and no other marks on my person. So, that's all I could come up with.

Miguel and I took some mini-trips. One to the beach, another to an amusement park. I was working for a hospitality organization and got really great deals on hotel and resort stays, so we took advantage of the good situations every chance presented us.

One night we even got engaged, but I contribute that to a night of heavy drinking—and petting—and some hopeful thinking on both our parts. We actually said some personal vows to one another, and considered ourselves "privately and personally" married.

Albeit I was head-over-heels for Miguel, I began to view our relationship as a dead end; I was truly hoping for something more serious, and long-term. He was showing extreme immaturity when it came to commitment, and either I was going to be first with him, or not at all. He had begun to slack off in that area, and I'd already been down that road too many times. I wanted maturity, commitment, and long-range plans. I wanted a man with a plan, not a boy who lived day to day. I'd been there, done that, and it wasn't working for me anymore. But, since I didn't have any alternate plan, I decided to let it ride and hope he'd grow up, soon.

~✝~

Because Miguel worked nights, he suggested I hang out with his best friend, Jack. Jack was awesome, and we became really good friends over the time I'd known him. Our relationship was always platonic; we just hit it off as friends who always loved a good party. He didn't have a girlfriend, and with Miguel always busy, that left a perfect situation for the two of us to be buddies. Well, perfect until one particular night.

Jack was always the designated driver, but he never was any good at it. After dancing the night away and enjoying the many drink specials, when it came time for us to go, Jack put the car in "drive", when he should have put it in "reverse". As he drove over the bushes in front of the car, the parking lot cop must have decided that was a really uncool thing to do. His lights went on, and within minutes, Jack was in the backseat of the cop's car, with me next to him. Jack got a DWI, and me, another PI. *Shit! Not again!*

A Public Intoxication never was any big deal for me; sort of like a parking ticket. I just hated being arrested and going to the police station, do paperwork, and feeling like a heel. A big inconvenience and party-buster it was. But, at least I wasn't the one with the big charge—-at least not this time, again.

Miguel was NOT happy about our news, and I was angry at him for being mad at me. Our relationship was spiraling out of control, and as young as our love was, it was dying, fast.

For several reasons, I enrolled in night classes. I needed to be productive with my evenings; that meant doing something to further my education and career, and to get my mind off my problems with Miguel. I was bitching at him for not having a purpose in life, but I needed to practice what I preached. And all was going well…for a while.

Working 40 hours a week and taking a full load of college courses in the evenings, I was feeling really good about myself. For the first time in my life I felt like I had control over my present and my future. Making straight A's in school, I was on top of the world and I was making some intelligent, goal-oriented friends.

After mid-term exams one evening, several of us decided to go to the club. There was a great local band playing close by, and we were needing to de-stress and celebrate our achievements. My friend, Winnie, promised she'd drive us. I was adamant about not driving after having been drinking, and she re-assured me she would be the responsible party that evening. But, she saw an old boyfriend at the club, and that was the last I saw of her that night; we were in *my* beautiful new car. She was so excited about driving it, or so she said. As pissed as I was, it didn't come close to the way I felt when some asshole ran into me on the way home, three miles from my apartment.

Of course, the cops came; of course, I was charged with driving while intoxicated. This time, being number 3, I had a felony on my record. *Fuck!*

As good as life had become, it turned rotten within a matter of moments. Now twenty-six and a convicted felon, I had no idea what would happen next. I was *very* scared, and *very* disappointed—in me

My lawyer was pretty good, he eventually got me probation for a few years. He was also a recovering alcoholic and addict. He once told me—in his office—that if he'd still been snorting cocaine, we'd be "screwing on my desk". I thought that was a pretty bold statement, but whatever. He was a caring individual and introduced me to a good AA group. I began to take sobriety seriously, well, a little, for a while. I still wasn't ready for the whole trip.

Miguel and I were now estranged; we both were rebelling in what was left of a dying relationship, although neither one of us ever formally "ended" it.

With attorney's fees piling up and Miguel's *non*-contribution to the bills, I needed to take on a semi-part-time job to pick up the slack. Another friend at school, knowing I had done a great deal of modeling, introduced me to Claire—the owner of an upscale, fancy ladies' boutique. She told me that beside the money I could make doing public fashion shows, playing the occasional guest-of-honor to her vast array of ritzy, private-party-going clientele would prove to be to my benefit. Little did I know that very soon, I'd would meet Lucifer, face-to-face.

CHAPTER 23

THE PARTY WAS ABUZZ...LITERALLY. LOTS of folks from the high-end tech world—geeks, business people, nerds of all flavors—highly-educated, and very much intoxicated. Wealthy folks high on alcohol, weed, cocaine and whatever else was floating through the air. I was there to do a "show", make some money, contacts, and enjoy the atmosphere. *Usually not a problem for me at this point.*

The venue was the lovely home of a married couple; friends of a friend, as so it was. I happened to make a fairly large profit that night, selling the glitz of gowns and nightwear for all that seduces you, or should I say, for those you want to seduce. I was one of Claire's best models—chic, shrewd, sexy and classy. She often chose me to show her top-selling items, and neither of us complained of the outcome. And for each naughty-but-nice item sold, I received not only a profit, but a large discount if I chose such item for my own armoire. Tonight, was no different.

"A what?" Did I hear her right?

"A swinger's party. Don't worry and don't be critical; they're all nice people, with nice pocketbooks, I promise." She promised.

I hadn't actually *been* to one of these, but I'd heard about them. I guess they weren't all that much different than what I was used to, or *were they?* Needless to say, I was going, and chose to take a couple of friends of my own, just in case I needed to make a quick get-away. Besides, I wasn't driving, and I needed their "chauffeurism". Anyway, they didn't have anything else to do on this particular Saturday night, and wanted to tag along to "see". Trust me—there was *lots* to see!

After my showing of frilly items and making various acquaintances, I was meandering about catching the "sights" when I noticed this guy, following me around—*all* around. I was at the bar; he was at the bar. I went to the hors d'oeuvres table, he followed me there as well. When I wanted fresh air, he was beside me on the terrace. A stalker—without discretion.

He didn't carry a leash, and I'd left the cuffs at home, so I figured he wasn't interested in the party-games being played that night. I decided to just stand there; perhaps he'll get tired of following me around like a wet dog looking for a home, and say something.

"Hello. I'm Richard. You put on a great show; loved the costumes. Are you friends of the host, or hostess?" He even *sounded* like a dog looking for a home. I was surprised he wasn't panting at me.

"Hi. I'm Marley. Thank you, and they aren't costumes. They're outfits. And to answer your rhetorical question; (I looked around) does it matter?" I tried to be nice. He was complimentary, in a way. Decent-looking, older guy. Apparently, I made a big impression on him, because everyone at the party from that point on thought we were "together". He never left my side. Oh well, he was attentive to say the least, and I wasn't interested in the orgy-like atmosphere in other parts of the house. Anyway, we passed some time with drinks and a joint.

When it was time to go, I gathered my friends to say "ta-ta". At Richard's persistence, I took his phone number—since I refused to give him mine—as he insisted I call him the next day. *We'll see what happens, I thought.* I was still mourning the death of my relationship with Miguel, and certainly wasn't about to get into another relationship, especially since I had no idea of my fate concerning my legal issues. *Yes, we'll see what happens.*

Bored and bummed the next afternoon, I reached in my evening jacket and pulled out a piece of paper. Richard "Dick" Natás. He didn't return my call for another day or two, but by the end of the week, we'd gone to lunch twice, and dinner three times. In fact, he was so sure of himself—and me, obviously—that he asked me to marry him that very first week. Not only that, but within the first month, he was paying my bills and had Miguel's name taken off the phone listing. Did I forget to mention he insisted I move in with him before we knew each other 3 weeks? I was beginning to find out just how persistent, and obsessive he really was.

But, could this be the guy I had been looking for? He was a "take control" kind of guy, apparently. He took the reins and I followed. Richard had an extreme education—the best money could buy, and was over twenty years my senior. Well-educated. Mature? Perhaps someone who would want the same things as I—a home, family, a successful and productive life? I was beginning to fixate my ideals in his corner. Besides, I suppose I was truly flattered. He was crazy about me, and, I mean, finally I found the qualities in someone I had been searching for—who wanted me as well. Or so I thought.

Richard was handsome, sort of. He had a good physique—for an older guy. About six feet one, large chest and shoulders; he was a workout fanatic. But his nose was crooked and his face pinched up. His eyes were deep-set, as if they sat in dark caves, but I was raised to look beyond the facade of a person, and see what's inside their soul. Had he been transparent, I would have learned he was the ugliest person on the face of the earth. Although I only knew him superficially now, I knew I'd get to know him as time progressed. However, as I did grow to know him, I found he had no soul. I found he was a demon on earth, doing the Devil's work.

CHAPTER 23

WE MOVED IN TOGETHER—I WITH him, to be honest. His apartment was larger, and a little more upscale than mine. After one week, his "contract" job ended, and at $7.50 an hour, I was supporting both myself *and* my new roommate—the one with the Ph.D. With doubts set aside, I was trying to complete the pretty package of the perfect man I'd always wanted, but this one wasn't closing. The qualities weren't fitting together in the same box. This especially true after he explained the "Wanted" posters pinned up all over the ritzy apartment complex.

"What on earth happened? Someone tried to bust through the security gate?" I asked, reading the flier requesting any information on the deviate who destroyed the electric, eight-foot, black wrought-iron security gate at the entrance to the complex.

He explained that after a night of heavy sex, drugs and alcohol, it was late when he was coming home. No one was in the little security house, naturally. Not being able to remember the security code, he backed up his older-model "man ride", and rammed into the gate, busting the lock. He got out, quickly opened the gate, and went on through. I could not believe what he was saying, but more than that, I was stunned that no one in the entire complex saw what happened, or even admitted to hearing something. This was very puzzling, and now I know why I called him "The Dick" from this point on.

~†~

"The Dick" and I continued on. He finally got a job doing whatever it was he did—I never totally understood all the technicalities of his technological skills, but that was his thing. I was glad to have his income coming in, and was committed to making a commitment—out of both of us. I didn't necessary love him, but he was being a near-normal person, and I was beginning to want to make sense of the future. As much as I suggested matrimony, he objected. I now know the truth about the saying, "*be careful what you wish for; you just might get it*".

Dick became increasingly more controlling, and I continued to stand my ground. But his manipulations of me weren't always so clear. Working, going to school, visiting my family when possible and going to church—alone—should have been enough for any man to be happy with his mate, but not this asshole. He began to check up on me when I went to the market, making snide remarks that I'd been "gone too long", or some off-the-wall stuff like, "I called the store, and they said they paged you. You never went." I was being accused of the most ridiculous sort of shit I'd ever heard of, but he'd apologize and all was good once again. I excused him for being a jealous, insecure, genius introvert. That sort of band-aided the bullshit, so I left it at that. Besides, after I looked at my relationship history, I realized I'd better count my blessings and accept that no man was the "ideal" man, at least not for me. (Mom once told me, "Marley, you have a bad picker".) This went on for some time.

But the good part of "The Dick" was that he was supportive of my sobriety. Three years to be exact. I attended AA meetings, and we went to restaurants that didn't serve alcohol. Although he said he'd love to have a cocktail now and then, he refrained, for my benefit. He knew I was on probation, and didn't want to jeopardize that in any way. Besides, as much as we worked out and ate healthy, there really was no time for alcohol, or any other recreational drug. We were both being randomly tested for drugs, so any euphoric moment wasn't worth the consequences.

I eventually got a good job as an alcohol and drug addiction counselor. Knowing, in depth, the effects of addiction and the lives it ruins, I was finally doing what I wanted to in life—help others. I believe that we are all here on this earth to help each other get from this life to the next, and with enough credits toward a degree in human services, I was able to get a job as a chemical-dependency addiction counselor. Now, life was pretty good, and for once, I was on the "other side of the fence".

CHAPTER 24

BY NOW, SISSY WAS ON her second and forever marriage. She'd caught the first asshole cheating with her slut of a best friend, so that finalized that one. But, when God closes one door, He opens another, and Door #2 turned out to be a winner for Sissy. Maurice, a great guy from the Coastal area, has always been a top-notch guy. They had a beautiful wedding of which I was, of course, maid-of-honor, but *this* time Sissy chose to keep their own top-tier of the wedding cake.

With Sissy's and Maurice's traveling the world, they were always getting great deals on vacation packages. Our trip on a Caribbean cruise was no exception. Mom, Sissy, and me, on a 7-day cruise to ports in Mexico and Jamaica. We had an absolute blast! Sober and memorable. *Hmm...vacation + sober = memorable. Imagine that!*

But, rarely is a trip taken that I haven't fallen in love with someone. This trip, it was a crew member. Georgios—a sexy, vibrant, handsome man from Greece. We had a blast on the ship. And an affair. Well, sort of. We never actually *had* sex, but we were intimate, and everyone—crew and passengers, looked upon us as a "couple". George told everyone he was in love with me. We danced, laughed, walked the decks, and made love—the way they did in the classic movies. We had fun, we were smitten. I'd told him of my controlling "roommate", and roommate is what Dick and I were during this time.

Georgios asked me to run away with him to Greece, but I couldn't bear the thought of living so far away from my family, and I was doing well with most aspects of my life, as well as working on a commitment to, and from, Dick. Anyway, with my luck in relationships, I was scared shitless of getting lost in a foreign land, alone, and heaven knows what else.

I saw my Greek friend a few times, however, when the Stella (our cruise ship) came back to dock at our coastlines. For a few years we kept in touch. He'd often call me, or Mom or Sissy, asking about me.

~†~

Dick and I were growing apart instead of closer, and I'd had enough. He was getting on my nerves more than ever, and the holidays were approaching. I wanted them to be a happy time, and with Dick hounding me as he did, I'd decided there'd be hell to pay if I didn't take that opportunity to move out.

After a great holiday ski trip with family members, I moved into a darling little place I'd found closer to where I was working and going to school. Finally, I could start over, *again*, in my precious new abode. We were cordial; Dick agreed to the move. *He even helped me move!*

But I'll be damned if the house Dick was playing solitaire in—the one I'd recently left—caught fire one day while he was at work, and burned to the ground. It was an old house, built in the war era, and an electrical shortage started, and never stopped. Had he not been at work, I wouldn't put it past him to start the fire himself, just to get under my skin. *Shit!*

"One month! You can stay ONE month, and that's ALL!" I was furious. Why couldn't he move in with someone else? But who? No one liked him, especially me, but I was his only resource, and with my motto of "helping others", well, what else could I do? So much for my new, exciting and independent life. *I could do anything for one month…*I reminded myself.

He actually did move in with some lady landlord—of course—but after one week, she kicked him out. *No one liked "The Dick"*! He was a loser, but more so an asshole, and we all knew it.

After about two months, I kicked him out. Of course, the only person who'd possibly let him move in was a woman, or so he said. But, being the man-whore, he was, I neither knew the truth, nor cared. I just wanted him out of my home.

After about a week, he called me during the middle of the night. "Can you come bail me out? I got a DWI tonight."

CHAPTER 25

SPRING OF 1992; I WAS doing great! Now working two jobs, a total of 85 hours each week including weekends, and taking on a full college schedule, I couldn't have been happier. While maintaining a 4.0 GPA and doing a counseling internship at a local adolescent rehabilitation center, I was also working my regular job as secretary at a national corporation; I couldn't have felt more independent and proud—and deservingly so.

Dick and I were still seeing each other, but dating others as well— *when I had a minute to do so.* He had gotten irate with me for going out with an "ex" of mine, and of course with no commitment, I really didn't give a damn. But, I guess you could say we were still "hanging on", and one night during a "make-up" session, well, I knew when it happened.

"Yes, Miss Thomson. The pregnancy test is positive." I had been to a clinic for a checkup and to confirm what I already was sure of. I was elated! Ecstatic beyond belief. Not that it was particularly *Dick's* child, but *mine!* I wanted this baby or than anything, and no one was going to stop me this time. There was no one in my way, and I was going to be a mom.

Weeks gone by, and knowing I was out of the danger zone for an early miscarriage, I asked Dick to come over and "talk". This would be the big night; the night he found out *we* were having a child.

I bought a cute card which comically explained to the prospective "father" that he was about to be one. "Uh oh," was all he said. His eyes looking like I'd turned into a fire-breathing dragon about to do damage. Stunned and disappointed, no doubt.

But after one comment of "What are you going to do?" I politely asked him to leave, and not bother me anymore.

"I'm going to be a mother, with or without you," I demanded. Then *he* demanded we seek counseling.

"For *what?*" I asked. "We're about to be parents...or at least *I* am." *No counseling needed, jackass.* That's when he threatened me with a lawsuit. Told me that if I didn't get rid of "that", as he pointed to my stomach, then he'd sue me—for what, he never said. And I was too overwhelmed to ask.

"I'll have nothing to do with either of you," he said with the arrogance of a conceited, manipulative, controlling, egotistical, male-chauvinist fucking *pig.*

"Get the hell off my property, and leave me the hell alone," I demanded as I shut the door in his face.

~✝~

"My grandfather is having open-heart surgery, *please* shut the fuck up! Gawd, I wish you hadn't come along." I was beside myself as we were driving to the hospital. Grandfather was about to be wheeled into surgery, and I wanted to get to him without any more drama than need be. I wanted to tell him that he was going to be a great-grandfather—I was so proud, and knew he would be, too.

As I held his hand, he smiled up at me when I told him the news. His sweet face showed happiness in its eyes. "You come live with your Grandmother and me." I leaned over and hugged him; told him I loved him. That was the last time I ever saw him, alive. *Rest in peace, my dear, sweet loving Grandfather.*

Dick was still being, well, just that. He'd actually been *fairly* decent to me once or twice, as I was lamenting the loss of my beloved granddad. But the night I went to his house and caught him in bed with another woman, I decided I was done.

He'd called me several times, pleading that I come to his house and talk about our "situation". He told me he was lonely, and wanted my company. I'd had round-the-clock morning sickness, and certainly didn't feel like putting up with his extraordinary bullshit. But when the nausea eased up a little, I decided to pay him his requested visit. What I found when I got there, I'll never forget.

High heels on the floor, mostly-emptied wine glasses on the coffee table, they were locked in the bedroom; Dick and whomever. I threw up on the panties by the shoes. Obviously, this sub-human had found someone, or some *thing* to ease his loneliness. I spent the next several hours listening to the "Marley, I'm so sorry…it's not what it looked like…" bullshit on my answering machine. Although we still didn't have a "commitment", I always found him to be a pompous jerk of the grandest kind.

I spent the next few months traveling back and forth to Bridgeton; spending as much time as possible with Grandmother and other family members. The position of secretary was no more, and I was now a full-time counselor intern and student. The family was taking good care of me and my unborn child, insisting I eat well, rest, and keep off my feet as much as possible.

Dick was changing his tune, and wanting to be more a part of my life and the baby's, so I issued an ultimatum: "If we aren't married when the baby arrives, he won't have your last name." I suppose that hit a nerve. Dick handed me his credit card and told me to go out and buy myself a ring. *Wow…that's true compassion.* But, what more did I expect from an asshole?

We had a lovely, small ceremony in Grandmother's (and Grandfather's, of course) home. Eight and a half months' pregnant, I finally got a commitment from "The Dick".

Fast forward a couple of years along with many bruises, false accusations, tremendous embarrassments and pure torture from a psychotic, jealous and overbearing asshole. And two gorgeous children I adored more than I ever thought possible. I'd quit my job, now focusing solely on being a mother to the most beautiful beings on earth. *How can someone be so happy, yet so miserable at the same time?* But when Dick began using our children as pawns to get me to do whatever it was *he* wanted me to do, I decided that was taking things to an all-time low, and *way* too far.

Following me around, sticking tape recorders in my face, just wanting me to touch him, or curse him out—which I was good at doing by this time. But, he was neglectful with the children; spending all his time taunting me. One time in particular Dick was working in the yard. He'd come in the house to holler at me for something, and left the door wide open. He was too busy harassing me to notice we had young children toddling throughout the house, and finally, into the yard. One passerby—in a vehicle, no doubt—brought my three-year-old to me via the garage. "I believe this might be your child?" he asked. I was furious! My precious baby had wondered out of the house, and into the street. Dick was a detriment to our family. *No wonder I have nothing but loatheness for this being.*

The ugly, nasty divorce went on for over a year. I ended up with sole custody of my children; Dick had been found guilty of family violence, due to his infidelity, neglect and abuse. But the kids and I settled nicely in Bridgeton; I decided it was best to move back near Mom and Dad, and my other familial support. Dick was going against all that was ordered of him, and I needed to be on friendly territory. Living near that monster was only making matters worse, for everyone involved.

CHAPTER 26

THE KIDS AND I WERE spending the final weekends of the summer near the beach, at Aunt Sissy's. We all loved the ocean and were getting in all the swim time possible, before buckling down to an autumn schedule. Then I got the call I never imagined would be. Miguel had been killed in a motorcycle accident. Driving home one evening from work, he didn't make the curve in the road as he should, and lost control of his bike. He'd been thrown head first into a hydrant.

Dear, precious Miguel; I'd spoken with him a few months earlier. Something told me to call him, and make amends. We hadn't spoken in a few years, but I needed to let him know I was all right, and inquired about his status, as well. We had a sweet conversation, expressed our everlasting love, and hung up. I never would have imagined I'd soon be attending his closed-casket funeral. The mother of his young son was the person who'd called me with the dreaded news. She also told me I was the love of his life; she knew he would want me to know. She said "I'm honored to speak to the person who held Miguel's heart". *Rest in peace, Dear Miguel.*

"The Dick" continued to taunt and harass, not only me, but my family members as well. He wanted me to come back to him; the more I rejected, the worse he got. Mother always called him "The Anti-Christ". That was mild compared to his reality. But, I continued on, striving to be a good mother, and work with Dick as best I could so the kiddos would still have a dad in their lives, no matter how I felt for him.

CHAPTER 27

THE GYM SCENE WAS THE one for me. With the muscle tone of a body-builder, I looked and felt the part of someone who was both physically and mentally fit. I put a tremendous effort in being of extreme form, and the end-product showed. Every curve of each tendon on top of muscle, on top of bone, my mind was reaping the benefits as well. I was doing all right.

Our small cottage-like abode was just perfect for a single mom and her precious cargo; it fit our family, and our budget. My part-time job and the money I was getting from the Dick was just enough for our quiet, fun lifestyle. We were doing well, and it showed. And as with the healthy living, comes the goodness from Earth's plants—marihuana, and that of natural juices— the *grape*. When the kids were at Mom's, or spending the weekend with their Dad, I was enjoying "me time" with the benefits of nature. *Life in all its glory.*

At 34 years old and a history of enough relationships to make Liz Taylor squeamish, I didn't have a man in my life, nor had any desire for one. I was concentrating on my little ones, my job, and the here and now. *But, isn't it funny how things change when we least expect it?*

I wasn't a social butterfly, but was interested in having a friend, or two. The church clubs offered didn't appeal to me, and the only people I encountered that were near my age, usually were those at the gym. Other than that, there was a couple with young kids down the street. Often, we'd get together, and enjoy each other's company, as well as a refreshment or two.

I joined a country club so we'd have a place to swim and hang out, until a local contractor decided to tear it down and make use of its land for somebody's parking lot. Then there was the lake; it was always a place to swim, picnic, and play some sort of ball. But, with my history of drinking and driving, those times were limited—*I'm ashamed to say.*

Other times we visited family, attended movie showings and ate out, or loaded up the suitcases and headed to the beach to visit Aunt Sissy. Her family was always fun to be around; there was always excitement to be had. We could spot an amusement park from miles away, or often attended the local fair with thrill rides and good food.

Maurice and Sissy owned a ranch way down south, just north of the border. We loved to go there for holidays or wintery weekends. Sometimes we'd camp out on the vast land, where we'd hunt for wild turkeys or deer, or fish for a variety of species of fish. We'd build a campfire that would last for days; sit around it roasting marshmallows, or tell tales of long ago.

Sometimes we'd cross the border into Mexico, shop for cheap deals and end up at a restaurant eating enchiladas and taking in some cold, homemade margaritas. One time our "designated driver" got lost on the way back, but we eventually made it to the camp safely, and in one piece.

But one Thanksgiving weekend, I hunted with Dad and killed my first deer. While looking out my bathroom window later that day, letting the cool autumn air filter away the smoke from my reefer, all I could envision when I looked at my "prize" was "the Dick"—hanging by his feet from a large tree. His entire body slashed, gutted, from crotch to face. Dead. Very dead. *Life was good…life was really good.*

CHAPTER 28

I HAD BEEN OUT ON dates a couple of times, but with no one I would want to ever remember. This one guy—I met him at the gym—was another egotistical, arrogant asshole. *By the time he's 45 he'll be fat, bald, and probably homeless; certainly friendless.* His idea of a date was me watching him devour a dozen scrambled eggs, one pound of bacon, and a gallon of milk. Then, I was forced to sit by him at a ballgame while he panted over every female that crossed our paths, and never once asked me if I was having a nice time. He didn't even have the decency to introduce me to any of his "friends". *What a jerk.*

When we got back to his apartment and he invited me in, he pushed me through the threshold and onto the sectional couch. After I fought off the assault of his trying to tear off my clothes, I pushed him away, and told him never to call me again.

The next day at the gym, he'd told a couple of trainers he'd "made it with me" the night before. Within one hour he was fired from his job, but not before I had a written apology in my hand. The manager of the gym—Barry—was a friend from long ago, and we had become re-acquainted. He was falling for me fast, and wasn't about to allow the little asshole to degrade me in any way. *I like the take-charge kind…well, sometimes. Correction: I like the "take up for me" kind of guy.*

Barry and I spent a lot of time together, at the gym, that is. He was a terrific work-out partner, and we laughed—a lot. He reminded me that long ago, during one night in another city where he was working the same fitness chain, I was shooting a commercial for said fitness chain.

"You were there?! Oh my gosh!" I had no idea. Guess I didn't notice him that night, what with Nico and all the excitement, but Barry let me know he sure noticed me.

"That's the night I fell in love with you, again..." he insisted. The first time was when I worked as an aerobics instructor, and he met me during a health fair, somewhere. I was working with Abbi that night at the fair, and I remember she invited the guys in the next booth to go out with us afterwards, to happy hour and whatever else. We did, and I'd given up any hope of ever seeing this guy again. Abbi had her sights on Barry, and she was way too aggressive for me to compete with. But here he was, professing his love to me, from times before when I had no idea. And I was falling for him as well, and fast. But there was one catch—he was a married man.

Barry told me about his marriage—his failing marriage. He wasn't happy, but didn't want to leave her. He'd made his vows, and insisted on playing the part of the responsible husband, but he was lying—to both of us.

"This is my third chance with you," he told me one night, "and I'm not letting this one by." With all the time we'd spent working out together or talking on the phone, laughing, neither one of us had an inkling as to how deeply involved we were about to get.

CHAPTER 29

THE CHILDREN WERE ON HOLIDAY, with, ok, *Richard*. I was seriously trying to be nice, or at least cordial, for all of our sakes. Chilling at my little abode, preparing for the coming days off, I was enjoying a little vino and some old-fashioned love songs, when the doorbell rang.

"Barry...what are you doing here?" I looked past him, toward the driveway. I honestly don't know what I was looking for; I was just shocked, I guess.

I let him know I was busy making plans for my family holiday. I was terrified to let him in—I knew I wanted to. But he told me he'd gotten hold of some really great smoke, and wanted to share a holiday reefer with me. *Shit...how could I possibly pass that one up?!*

So, we smoked, drank a toast (or three or four), and within moments it seemed, he was reaching for the back of my neck, pulling me toward him, kissing me with the passion lovers often do.

"I can't do this, Barry; not with you wearing that ring." As it wasn't my intent, our clothes came off that evening, but not before he slipped off the gold band.

Of course, Barry explained his marital misery. Of course, their marriage was one of convenience. Of course, he went on to say he wasn't in love with his wife; the object of his affection was me. And I had fallen into the pit of lust and love as well, and hit its bottom with a vengeance.

~†~

Barry was becoming an ornate object at my home. When he wasn't working, he could be found at my home, even by his wife. *Awkward, but true.* Sometimes I even wondered if perhaps he wasn't married—we were together so much. I wondered what sort of "set up" they had; did she know where he was? Did she care?

My home was his home; he adored my children and they were crazy about him. He called me "his wife". We were living in a dream world— *our dream world*. We were inseparable, and desperately in love.

We drank, and smoked, and drank some more. Wherever we were, so the party was. We laughed, loved, and laughed some more. And then we'd love, lust, and love again. Constantly stoned to the beat of our addictive personalities always in sync. Were we so much alike that we just loved to be high together, or were we living a lie—a dream, a fantasy— that could only be real *if*, and *when*, we were stoned? We couldn't drink enough wine or smoke enough pot to keep up with our urges and cravings. And we couldn't laugh and love enough, at least in the beginning.

But the double-life caught up with him. Barry began to realize his responsibility to his *real* wife, and he was troubled. He started putting crushed up sleeping pills in my wine when I wasn't looking, so I'd pass out late at night. When I'd wake and find him gone, I felt deserted, and so alone. Sure, he'd hold me until I fell asleep, then he'd sneak out and go to his own bed, *her* bed. He promised they weren't sleeping together; he loved only me, and he would *fix it*, once and for all. He insisted he was going to ask her for a divorce. Over and over, I heard that. Over and over, we began to fight. I told him so many times "It's over, Barry!", but he always came back, and I always took him.

We'd plan a wedding date, but their divorce didn't go through. Then, we'd plan another, but again, no divorce. This went on for months, and they'd turn into years. I was stupid—stupidly in love. But I knew he loved me, and trusted his intentions. Barry did leave his wife, more than once, but she'd beg and plead like a pathetic desperado until he caved.

"She needs me; she doesn't have anyone else. You have your family." Then he'd get sucked back in to living a miserable existence. That's the way he described the scenario to me many times throughout our lucid affair. Finally, I had enough. I realized that if he couldn't commit to me now, if he ever did, she'd always be in the balance. I wasn't ready—never would be—to share any man, with any other woman. I was done; we were done.

"Marley, I love you. Please, please don't give up on us!" He begged. He pleaded. He followed me one weekend to Coastal Bay, where I went to visit Sissy and her family. I needed the break from my domestic doom, and the beach was just the ticket to put space between Barry, and myself. But when Maurice answered the door one very early morning with a gun in his hand, I knew Barry had truly gone overboard.

"I need to see Marley, please," he begged Maurice. It was past 3:00 a.m., and I'd been asleep in the guest room. I could hear the conversation.

"Marley is asleep, and you need to leave...*now,*" demanded Maurice. "If you don't leave, I'm calling the police." With the show of iron in his fist, Maurice needn't say any more.

The next day, as I was frolicking in the waves of the ocean, I felt eyes on me—*more so than usual.* I turned around toward the Boulevard, scanned the premises, and saw him. Barry was sitting in his car, watching me. *What the hell?!*

We talked. He cried. I cried. We talked some more. "I'm getting counseling, Marley. I need to let you know that I can't live without you, but I can't leave her, either." Well, something had to give, and it was going to be me. I wasn't about to live life in a threesome—the only threesome I was interested in living in was that of my own two children, and me. That's all the room there was for me in life, I decided. Barry and I could try to be friends, if possible, but that would be the extent of our relationship.

We tried being friends; we really did. Now and then, on a lovely day—when the kids were with "The Dick", Barry and I would decide to take a country drive. We both loved nature, and liked the idea of getting out of Bridgeton via way of winding, rural roads. He knew the territory well, and as we always had before, loaded the cupboard-on-wheels with coolers of wine and bags of pot, and head out for the day by a lake or river, or a field of wild flowers miles away from civilization.

One beautiful Autumn day we were driving through the country-side, laughing like we did, never caring about the rest of the world. That was, until we came over a hilltop and met a sheriff's car coming toward us in the other lane. We were going well over the speed limit, but with the music and laughter so loud, we weren't paying attention; we never realized the speed. And perhaps we were swerving—that's what the sheriff told Barry, after he took us in to the local jail. Barry was charged with a DWI; I didn't get a PI, but was warned I should have. I guess when Barry's wife drove the 65 miles to bail him out, the sheriff had pity on me.

"That guy you were with, he's gone. His wife came to pick him up." *You poor, stupid dumb, bitch*— I'm sure he was thinking. I suppose it was to my advantage though, that day. Thank God, we had been in my car. I drove home, alone. Alone again…naturally. *I hated him. God, I hated him.*

Barry came over the next day. He wanted to apologize. I wanted to kill him, but the tranquilizers I was living on helped me not to care. We shared a joint and a bottle of wine, and decided that we'd always love each other, but we would never end up together. I told him if he was a Native American, his name would be "Running Back", because he kept running back to her, then me, and back and forth, and back and forth. He thought that was funny; I didn't. I hadn't "settled" for a second-rate relationship at this point in my life, and I wasn't going to do so now. Yes, I tried and tried—I was a hopeful person—but it was time to let go.

Proverbs 3:5 says: *Trust in the Lord with all your heart, and lean not on your own understanding…* and so I did.

A few rockier patches to climb, and a few more sinkholes to get around, but I knew that it was time to wave the white flag.

CHAPTER 30

INTERNET DATING WAS ALL THE rage, and I decided to give it a whirl. I hadn't gone out with a guy since the devastating break-up with Barry. Instead, I put forth my focus on building a country home for my little family of kids, cats and hamsters. We were happy; very happy. Our home was just that, *ours,* and we were doing well.

After putting the kids to bed, late at night I'd rock, peacefully, on our large front porch. On occasion, I'd see Barry drive by down the country dirt road which surrounded our home, or I'd find flowers on the doorstep early in the morning. Sometimes his signature empty beer can would find its way on my gravel drive, and in a strange way, my heart would smile. I knew he still loved me.

Dick was still and ever-growing thorn in my side, and being out in the fresh, country air was just the thing that helped me through trying, difficult days with the kids' dad, ex-lover(s) and future hindrances.

But with so many other yahoos in the world, I decided it was time to try the dating scene, once again. Especially when the kids were with Dick, I wanted to do things; have fun with someone special. Not that I wanted to be in love; I didn't. But I wanted friends to go out with, dance, and do things I liked to do, only not alone.

Love-on-the-Internet was where I put up my profile. I included a beautiful picture, and just enough information about myself to attract the educated, working professional, but not so much to attract everything that walked and breathed. I was specific in my likes and the not, and cautious about the inquiries I answered.

Delcie was the receptionist of our family business; I was the office manager. *Great job*! She was near my age, and single, wild and free—much like myself. We played on that damned computer so much, it's a wonder we ever got any work done…but we did. Work came first, of course, but we squeezed in plenty of fun from the internet whenever we could. And we had a system. When one of us was going to actually meet a guy, we'd set up a "lunch date". That way, we would both go, the "date" was at a public restaurant and time-limited, and we could offer each other our opinions. We met a plethora of men—young, old, handsome, not-so-handsome, fun, boring, and of as many professions as there were personalities. I dated a commercial pilot from San Antonio, Sammy—a fun and sexy lawyer from Houston; we had some wild times together at the coast—and I was crazy about this guy from California. I don't recall his name, but he was a movie producer, and offered to take me to Hawaii; said he was producing a "Wild Kingdom" type documentary, and wanted to spend time with me. We talked via video chat, a lot. He was cool, and I liked him. But, sometimes we'd be talking and he'd tell me his girlfriend in the other room was waking up. *Uh oh…* I wasn't about to become another long-distance homicide statistic, and get involved with pissed-off, jealous girlfriends.

And there was the professional basketball player—he liked to snort coke and talk on the phone to his buddies about me. He was "enthralled" that I was a model—loved my long legs and catwalk strut. He talked so much *about* me, that he hardly ever talked *to* me. Then there was the NFL player from Buffalo. I even met his daughter and his parents one night. They were real sweet, but he was beginning to get serious, and I wasn't about to take on a new "step-child". I would have had to move out of state, too, and that wasn't going to happen. I had my little family, and we had a lovely home. Plus, I was close to Mom and Dad, and my job was rockin'.

But I really became cautious about who I was befriending after one guy—a guy from the northern part of the state—came down to meet me. He was NOTHING like his profile, and yellow lights started going up around me everywhere. I was reminded of the Brad Paisley song about "Internet…" something or other. This guy took the term "internet fraud" to a whole new level. Anyway, by now, I couldn't keep up with all the guys wanting to chat, call, email, and meet, and I was getting tired of the "game". Sure, it was fun for a while, but I wasn't seeing anyone in particular, and didn't want to "date around". Then I met Walker.

CHAPTER 31

WALKER WAS A TEXAS COWBOY through and through, and my newfound friend. He was a local businessman—made all his money in long-time family real estate, and was an only child. Had no children, too. *That was a plus, no doubt.* Walker had a cute, sort of sexy way about him, even though he was a little wiseacre. I guess his smart-alecness was one thing that made me laugh, and we laughed—a lot. He owned a large, beautiful ranch, plenty of horses—my first and true loves—and we began to date exclusively right away. I'd posted a pic of me atop my Appaloosa on my internet profile; Walker told me it was my love for horses and my long, blue-jeaned legs that caught his eye. He was about fifteen years my senior, and had been married several times. We had a lot in common; then we found out we both loved to drink. *Not so good a thing in common.*

~✝~

Our first date—lunch. Delcie bailed on me at the last minute, and I was furious. "You can't do this to me, Delcie! What about our deal?" I was begging. I liked this guy, Walker, but it was our rule not to go meet any internet guys alone. But, one of the guys Delcie was crazy about had called at the last minute and asked her to lunch. She couldn't pass him up, and I couldn't compare to what he had to offer—*even at lunch.*

It was a very hot August afternoon. As usual, I had on a sundress—cool and sexy. This one was light blue with teal, squiggly vertical stripes, with splashes of yellow throughout the think cotton material. From the hips to the knees, the fabric was sort of kerchiefed—looked like the flap brushes in a modern carwash. Cork-wedged white sandals had just enough of a summer heel to accentuate my long, slender legs, and feminine ankles. *I was looking chic, as usual.*

I knew when I saw the four-door dooly taking up half the parking lot, that my lunch date had arrived. We hugged, talked, and laughed through the entire hour. Walker explained his love for hunting, and asked me to accompany him on an upcoming trip to Montana. Though I didn't want to get that far with someone I'd just met and really didn't know, I was intrigued with another trip he was talking about—a week-end journey to a guided, exotic animal hunt. It would be in a few weeks, and I was sure we'd know each other better by then. So, I told him, "… we'll see".

Walker had an ego to go with his charm and crackpot attitude. Later, I'd realize he was a very insecure, unhappy man, wearing a façade that could fool everyone in his world. I was one of those persons. *Why do we, as humans, fall for the façade of "nice guy"? How can we let ourselves be so fooled?*

The next Saturday, Delcie, her kids, me and mine, were all invited to his ranch, for a day of riding horses, hiking, and bar-be-cue. The ranch-house was two-story Austin Stone, and sat atop a large hill, overlooking miles of rolling hills. Treetops were everywhere; they looked like broccoli tops standing on end. There was even a rolling brook at the end of the property, and as I walked in that first time, I turned to Delcie and said, "This will all be mine, some day." I was as surprised as she was, but I felt it. I just knew. It wasn't out of a feeling of financial greed, but I've always been able to express a premonition, or sixth-sense of some sort. I had that feeling this day.

The menagerie of residents was greeted with open arms from all the kids that day. There were dogs, cats, horses; even a Billy-goat. I spotted some wild deer, and a fox later that evening. Oh, and an owl was perched on top of the weather vane at one point. It was all so warm and inviting, so natural, and blithe.

I was in my element, and riding like a champ. All the horses were special—all horses are special—but Fury was a spectacular prize. Standing tall, black and bold, this stallion was sturdy, tempered, and proud as a king. And a challenging ride, for me. I loved him; he reminded me of my first horses.

CHAPTER 32

ALL THE YEARS AS A little girl, wishing for my own horse had finally paid off. Probably, because Mom and Dad got so tired of me begging and pleading so often. I wanted a horse more than I wanted to live. When I was about twelve, they found some old farm hand wanting to get rid of a pasture horse. So, he became mine—*the pasture horse, not the farm hand.*

Being the first person ever on his back, he let me know he wanted me to be the last. Pepper was his name, and he threw me so many times I couldn't count. With emergency bills adding up periodically, Mom and Dad let it be known it was time to get rid of Pepper. So, we did, and I cried.

The next wild ride my family chose for me was a little tamer; I was about sixteen by now. Rocket was a good name for him; he, too, threw me off almost every time I saddled up. But eventually one of us would give in, and sometimes I'd win the fight.

Grandfather had the idea that if he brought Rocket into town one year, Mom and Dad would let me keep him in the back yard, and I could ride him in the rodeo that week, near the house. He did and we did, but Rocket tore up our beautiful back yard like nobody's business; I think Daddy wanted to turn Rocket into glue that year. That was a week of my youth I'll never forget, and probably neither will Dad. Rocket never was allowed to come back into town after that.

So, then there was Sundance. I adored Sundance. He belonged to a friend, who kept him at the rodeo site near the house. She allowed me to "adopt" Sundance, and I rode him constantly. Every afternoon, after school, I went to ride Sundance. Sometimes I just hung out with him; he was my pride and joy. I showed him in Western Pleasure shows; we rode in parades, rodeos, all around wherever we could. Sundance was a prince of a horse; an auburn and blond roan standing seventeen hands high. He was as tough a creature that ever walked he earth, and he was fast as lightning. He and I were a team—a power in the wind. We both felt so much freedom when we'd ride. He had an incredible spirit, and I loved him so; he knew that, too. And Fury reminded me of him greatly.

~†~

The next few months were sort of bumpy for Walker and me, but we were having fun traveling the horse-show circuit, and doing what we did best—drink and make merry.

Whatever we did, it was first class all the way, and Walker made sure of it. Often, after showing the horses all day, we'd hunker down in a nice hotel, complete with happy-hour and all the fixin's of an upper-class lifestyle. Sometimes, we'd wander to the nearest honky-tonk, listen to some real old-fashioned country & western music and dance the box— Walker was a great two-stepper as well. Howbeit, I began to notice a jealous streak when we'd be on the dance floor, especially when dancing separately. Seemed like the more he'd drink, and the more I'd "jig", the more arrogant he'd become. Once he accused some of my moves as "slutty"; he'd had quite a bit to drink, and I was getting some smiles from my dance colleagues. We were all just having a good time, at first.

Another time—over the holiday period—he took me hunting exotic animals on a ranch in far West Texas. He had some friends who owned the place, and it was truly remarkable. Black horn bucks, mule deer, bobcats and wild turkey—an array of wild life amongst beautiful, desert hills.

Our cabin was lovely; a stone fireplace and a picture window looking at the gorgeous multi-colored western sunset. Such a sight to behold. But there was one problem; it was next door to another cabin—with a *man* in it; a single, younger, easy-on-the eyes kind of man.

I certainly didn't flirt; I was with Walker. Anyway, I wasn't interested anyone else. I loved him, and we were talking marriage as of late. But Walker didn't like the way our neighbor said "Hello, how are you?" In fact, Walker didn't like the way *any* man talked to me; didn't want anyone else to breathe around me, I suppose. He figured all men should dry up and die as soon as they got within looking distance of me, and *especially* if he'd ingested whiskey of any sort. The trip had some bad turns, but ended up being all right. Nevertheless, I did get pissed off enough that I sat in the back seat of the truck all the way home, and it was a *very long* drive back home. Walker locked me in the truck, and wouldn't let me out until I heard his long apologies and undying love. Of course, he was sorry, and of course, he loved me *so* much. "Blame it on the alcohol…", he said. So, I did.

Since it was the holiday season, Santa came around and was *very* good to me and the kids. *Very good.* The kids each got game sets and new televisions for their rooms, and I got the biggest, gold and diamond engagement ring I'd ever seen. It was almost gaudy. But it was beautiful—gorgeous, actually. I recall it being so big that I wasn't quite sure if Walker gave that to *me*, or to *his self.* He could be quite showy, and show-off he did. He proposed, and I accepted. God, how in hindsight we realize we should have done things differently. But I knew—even though he and I had our problems, especially when we drank—he could give us the life we deserved, and never have to worry about finances, again. My children deserved it, and so did I. I would put up with his menial bullshit, for the good of my family. Sounds terrible now, but that's not the way it started out. I did love him, and the kids liked him, too. He was a kidder, and enjoyed them immensely. They were the only children he had ever had. He liked to spoil them, and I liked him spoiling them, too. I wanted them to have everything they ever wanted, and this man could, and would give it to them. *I thought.*

Our wedding was very quiet, in a small country chapel. Walker had wanted to be married in Spain, but after talking with the Spanish

Embassy and the Consulate in the States, we decided against it. Mother actually pleaded with me not to marry Walker in another country. "If you need to get out of it, it could prove to be almost impossible…" Mother said. Obviously, she had a premonition, which turned out to be oh, so correct.

CHAPTER 33

WE WERE ARGUING CONSTANTLY. WHETHER I was talking to the boy at the check-out stand in the supermarket, or looking at the passer-by in the mall, I was accused of cheating. Constantly, Walker was on my ass about looking at other men, talking to other men—*enticing other men*.

"What the fuck am I supposed to do? Ignore the entire human race? We don't live *that far out* to be considered hermits." I professed.

One time he looked at me and said "Slut"; I was laughing with the plumber on the phone, while making an appointment. Little did Walker know that the person I was talking to was a woman, but I never told him that. *Let him worry.* Maybe he'll worry so much, he'll have a heart attack and pass out…*way out!*

I was seriously getting sick of his shit; I'd pack some things to leave, and he'd grab my arm enroute to the doorway, kiss me, and apologize. Then he'd hand me a wad of hundreds and tell me "…buy you something nice…". He was always handing me money, and that helped, for a while. After the kisses, apologies and money, we'd drink. We'd *always* drink. It was a quick fix, for a long-term disaster.

But one night, his "arm-grabbing" was a little too harsh, and he went a little too far. He swung me around so hard, I felt my neck snap. The next thing I knew his entire hand—rough, working hand—went across my face so hard that I was thrown into the sheetrock. WHAM!! The dent in the sheetrock fit my head, exactly. But it wasn't a complete hole until the second WHACK!! Obviously, Walker wasn't satisfied with the first blow to my head. The hole was about one centimeter from the 2x4 boards making the doorway. Thank God, he stopped after realizing what he'd done. *I didn't know if it was me he was worried about, or the new hole in our lovely walls.* I was seeing stars and shapes I never knew existed. I could see colors of all sorts; it was like looking through a kaleidoscope. It was pretty, but I sure as hell wouldn't suggest seeing things that way.

I stumbled to find my keys while the stars finished dancing around in my head. I reached up to see if I was bleeding, but I wasn't. *That was a good sign, I think.* I got in my Jeep, and took off.

The narrow, unfinished country road was slick from the late night's dew, and my mind was teetering. My eyesight was unfocused; I was traumatized, and in shock, but I had to get out—to save my own life. I didn't know where I was going, but I had to get to safety—wherever that was.

All of a sudden, I felt as though I was on a roller coaster with my eyes closed. I was rolling, tossing, all around my vehicle. *Oh, Dear God… what's happening!!!?* It was all happening so fast; it—whatever it was. And then it stopped. I stopped, and I was upside down. Everything was dark. Silent. *What just happened? How did it happen?*

I could see my new flip-phone, just above my head; it was on the ground, lying on the top of my Jeep. Everything was so distorted. *"ET" called home; it was the only number I knew to call, especially out where we were.*

"Walker…?!"

"Yeah, Baby…I'm so sorry. Please come back home."

"Walker…I've had a wreck; a horrible wreck."

I could tell in his voice he thought I was making up a bad scenario to make him feel like shit.

"Baby, please, just come back home." He pleaded.

"I can't! Please, just come get me, damnit!" I cried.

The next thing I knew, I could see light.

"Marley!! Marley!! Oh my God! Marley!! Are you ok?!" Walker was frantic, and I could hear his footsteps in the leaves and brush, rushing toward me. Then they became distant, then close, again.

"Marley, close your eyes. Cover your eyes!" He demanded. Then, THUD! THUD!

I heard the crackle of glass; he had broken the front windshield with the butt of his pistol—the one he carried in his truck. I don't know how he did it, but he pulled me through.

I had had a blowout, causing my small SUV to fishtail. Then a tire caught the jagged edge of the unfinished country road. I went soaring somersault after somersault until the front end landed—engine first—causing the final flip in the ditch alongside the road.

I was all right, other than cuts and bruises, and a devastated self-esteem. Walker fixed us some much-needed, very strong toddies.

Later that week, the man at the wrecking yard told me my tires had been slashed.

~†~

Another night, another fight. This time, my head could not penetrate the solid wood our horse barn was made of.

Walker thrusted me twice, with his huge hands squeezing my shoulders, against the stall walls. We had promised each other we'd stop drinking, and the pot would go, too. But when I found his stash in the tack room, I became furious. He had been drinking, as well.

I knew it was a win/lose, for him and me, respectively, so I tried to walk away. I needed to go in the house, and deal with him, later. He became angry that I wouldn't talk to him, and was walking away, again. I wasn't about to put up a fight, especially since I knew he'd been drinking his favorite—whisky. But, once again, his strength won over my lanky awkwardness.

By the third thrust, I could imagine my bloody brains seeping down the barn walls. I'd been through similar situations, and wasn't about to go there, again. I began fighting back as hard as I could, scratching, kicking, yelling the most vulgar names at him that would come out of my mouth

His drinking got us in that situation, but it got me out of it, as well. He stopped fighting me, called me a few choice dirty words I'd gotten used to by now, and went back to his whisky and pot. I was able to run in the house, grab my purse and keys, and take off—once again.

~†~

The kids had been spending more and more time with the grandparents they adored. I didn't want them subjected to this situation, and needed to decide what to do next. Besides, they'd let me know in specific terms that the country was "boring", and I adhered to their wishes to spend more time in town with their grandparents. I just wanted them to be happy, and safe. I also knew that Walker would never hurt them physically, but hurting me *was* hurting me, and I needed to make some decisions. Anyway, they were getting enough mental and emotional anguish from "The Dick"; *they didn't need any more shit from either of these assholes.*

I began going back to my AA meetings, and to church. These places were where I needed to be—with sober people, Christian people, people I needed to be around. Grandmother had recently passed away, and I was spending more time with Mom. The family was devastated, and we missed her terribly. But I was sober, and surrounded myself with positive, helpful people. I also moved into the guest house, and told Walker I was filing for divorce.

CHAPTER 34

RIGHT BEFORE SCHOOL BEGAN, MY children suddenly decided they wanted the big city life instead of country living. They were liking Walker less and less, and Dick was only exaggerating the situation by filling them with stories—lies—one after another. He was also filling their little heads with the goings on between Walker and I—things they never would have known, nor should have, had Walker not told Dick. What I found out later—unbeknownst to me at the time—was that Dick had conspired with Walker to get the kids away from me, any way they could. Dick resented me for leaving him, and wanted my children away from me out of pure revenge; Walker wanted me for his own.

I was beyond devastated. After filing for divorce, I told myself I would stay with Walker and make him pay—in every possible way—for what he'd done to me, and my precious family.

By the grace of God, I remained sober through family, friends and faith. I leaned on my faith in God now, more than ever. He was the only way I could handle the duo of extreme evil-doers who had manipulated and intruded not only in the little bit of happiness I had in my life, but also in the precious lives of the very ones who provided that happiness. I needed a serious break, and to untangle the mounted mess of emotions I had incurred over the past year or so.

The deceit, the betrayal, and abuse of various sorts had overwhelmed every part of my being; I needed to round-up, gather or figure out any possible thoughts I might have about what the hell had been happening and what I would do from here. I hated Walker *almost* as much as I loathed "The Dick". I despised them both, but Dick was still somehow in the lead.

~✝~

September 11…a day of hell, for so many. *God rest the souls of the victims and the lives of their loved ones. God bless the lost, and the affected.* The most tragic day, for so many lives. A horrific day in my own.

Walker had been out of town for two, glorious weeks. Actually, he'd been in Africa on another exotic hunting trip. My days were free from bruises, accusations of infidelity, and ugly, disgusting remarks. *We had been to counseling several times, but Walker accused me of crossing my legs inappropriately during one session. The counselor was a male, of his choosing. I refused to go back after that.* I was enjoying the peace of life, at home without Walker.

On several occasions, I invited my AA friends out for riding, food and fellowship. I was enjoying sober living and freedom from the demon with whom I lived. I was taking every day at face value, making the best of my unhappy situation. Then he came home.

As I did every morning before work, I was sitting at my dresser fixing my face and hair, when I heard the horrible, ungodly news of terrorism in our nation. At work, we sat glued to the television set with dumbfounded thoughts and broken hearts. Our feelings were numb.

But I had errands to run, and even had to pick up some medication for Walker; he'd come home with terrible malaria-like symptoms, thought he was dying. He sat up all night in the easy-chair, unable to rest.

I drove around the lake, just thinking, enjoying the warmth of the sun through the sunroof of my new car. Walker was mad at me for purchasing it. He knew I needed it due to my Jeep being totaled, but the fact that I didn't "allow him to help in the choosing and purchasing" just about killed him. I actually made a purchase—and a deal—without him. He was pissed, and, well, he was just pissed at me, period. He hated the world right now, and I hated him. I didn't want to go home to a big, lonely house with a sick, grumpy asshole in it, but that's where I eventually headed.

I walked in the house at 5:35 pm; the news of the day's tragedies was on our big-screen television. He was slouched in the big comfortable, leather easy-chair in our Austin-stone living room, high on whatever Rx he'd already been taking, and booze—his favorite and my worst—whiskey.

He repeatedly asked me where I'd been after work, and what all I'd done the two weeks he was gone. Pretty much, he wanted the synopsis of each moment of every breath I took while not in his presence, and I was getting really irritated. What I didn't know was that he hired our drunk neighbor—of all people—to spy on me while he was gone. God only knows what all the neighbor told him… apparently about seeing other people at our home. *Not good—whatever it was.*

As I frustratingly began reiterating my every move over the last two weeks—including this awful day—I looked into his eyes, and realized that whatever was in there, wasn't human. Although I'd already met "Lucifer", I was definitely looking into the eyes of one of his demons. It was wicked, and scary. Sweat was running down his face, and I swear I could see fire coming out of every exposed orifice. If looks could kill, I'd have been mutilated by this human Tommy-Gun.

"If you want me to take you to the E.R., I will. Otherwise, I'm not going to sit here and do this." My peace had been invaded, and I wasn't having any more of his bilious rubbish.

"You're not going anywhere, Bitch," he said as he tossed his blanket away from his self. He was headed my way.

I was one step ahead of him as I grabbed my keys, and headed for the door. Although I was in my car within a matter of seconds, he was already there, it seemed. As I was trying to get the key in the ignition with my shaking hand, he reached through the open sunroof, and grabbed a huge handful of my long flowing hair. His grip was covering the roots of my skull, and his entire strength was set on scalping me. I literally could feel my scalp lifting from the bone of my skull, and as I grabbed his arm with both of my hands, I scratched and clawed with every ounce of strength I had. I was screaming as loudly as my voice could carry, yelling for help—anything that could save my life.

Walker's extremely tight grip wasn't loosening, and I wanted to lay my hands on the horn; make any amount of noise I could. But he had such a tight grip on my scalp, and pulling harder with every second, that I couldn't take my hands off of his arm. The pain was intolerable, and all I could think about was how the Indians used to scalp people, tearing their heads off their bodies. I felt my head was coming apart, and I was scared shitless; screaming and fighting like a maniac.

All of a sudden, I was being dragged out of the car—by my hair, through the sunroof. Like a ragdoll, I passed through the hole in the top of the car, and onto the concrete floor of the driveway. I landed on my back, and Walker got on top of me, straddling my tense, yet limp body. With both hands, he began beating my face and my chest. I didn't want to die this way, but thoughts of death were seemingly inviting. *God… somebody…. please help me! Was I in one piece? Was my hair on my head, my head on my body?* I was fighting for my life at the hands of, and underneath this sick, jealous, deranged fucking lunatic!

He stopped. Did he realize he was trying to murder his wife? Had his illness taken over, or was it the drugs and alcohol he'd consumed that day? Or was he so worn out by torturing me, beating me up that he'd used up all his might?

Did my survival instincts and rushes of strength take over, causing me to push, throw him off of me? I got up—in one piece—and ran like hell. I ran so fast, and so hard. Into the darkness…the very quiet darkness…into the country night.

CHAPTER 35

THE NEXT FEW DAYS WERE spent in a hotel. I'd gone back to the house and gathered some things; Walker had gone back to work. I called in sick, of course.

The nation had just experienced true tragedy and trauma, and in my own little world and insignificant life, so had I. Bruised, broken, and getting seriously drunk, I sat in the open doorway to my room, staring at the dingy, mossy green and brown water of the swimming pool—now closed for the season. Drinking, and drinking, I waited for Barry. I needed a friend; a hug. I wanted someone to hold me. I wanted Barry there, to make it all better. I wanted someone to drink with me, and get me high. But someone I knew could stay with me a while, then leave. I needed to be alone.

I never filed charges on Walker. He knew the local sheriff and all his deputies. In fact, he rode with a couple of them; they smoked dope together.

Walker always carried a large amount of cash with him, and never failed to let the local officers know they could depend on him for support of donations, and whatever else sort of shit crooked lawmen and their citizens did to woo the public. Anyway, my family had spent the last ten years dragged through the court crap with Dick and me, and I just wanted to get a quiet divorce. I filed, and moved out.

Of course, he begged and pleaded, and begged and pleaded. He bought me bigger diamonds, and more of them. I got a new car—one he picked out and paid for with cash. He began going to church with me, often. I made sure he bought everything my children wanted. *Break out the cash, asshole.*

Although I know so well that money can't buy happiness, I was using this fucking jerk for everything he was worth, and that was a decent amount. He'd caused me and mine true heartache; I'd already lost my children—thanks to him and "The Dick", so I didn't really have anything else to lose. I'd sold my country home and paid off all debts, and wasn't about to scrape by and do without, not as long as this son-of-a-bitch was around.

~✝~

For some very odd reason, we began to get along. Perhaps it was through prayer, or the counseling sessions with the Priest. Maybe it was because both of our lives were so messed up, and we were both tired. I threw in the towel at happiness; I didn't know where to go from here.

One day he told me that because he was adopted as a child, he had never felt a sense of belonging. He said he had always felt "lost"; like he was a "nobody". I'll never forget the sad, tearful look in his face as he told me this, and at that moment I truly felt sorry for him. All of his insecurities now had a reason for being. No one is perfect, and I made up my mind to deal with our situation as best I could, at least until I decided what to do further. I was tired, lost, and lonely.

CHAPTER 36

WE WEREN'T TOGETHER ON OUR first anniversary. As I was leaving him a card, I picked up the one he'd left me, next to the neatly gift-wrapped, small box. *What a tumultuous, horribly fucked-up year! Could I please have a do-over?* I wanted to go back two years, when I began internet dating, and NOT! But we were doing what we could to get along. I suppose if one lonely heart deserves another, we were in the right place, just at the wrong time.

Walker promised to stop drinking—he was just smoking pot now. I had booze stashed in every shoe, every pant pocket, every dirty-clothes hamper we had. Wherever I knew he wouldn't be, I had booze hidden.

Spring had sprung, and early summer was here. We were invited to an anniversary party of some of my nearest and dearest friends—a couple I hadn't seen in a while. They wanted to see me, and meet my new(est) husband. They'd known Ray, Miguel and Dick, and were a little anxious and skeptical—as they should be—about "what" I dragged into my life this time. Besides, they wanted to show off their beautiful new home in the lovely hill country—not far from where I used to live.

Walker made it very clear that the horse he wanted to buy some two-hundred miles away couldn't wait, and that he wouldn't be "accompanying" me to my friends'. The particular breeders obviously needed or do their business on the very weekend we'd been asked to the party, or did they? I made it clear that it was *his choice,* then made my hotel arrangements.

~✝~

The weekend came, and I was ready to roll. After pleading with Walker once more, I finally gave up and bid my farewells. He was leaving shortly after me, on that very beautiful spring Friday afternoon.

Upon arrival at my hotel, I called my friends to let them know I had made it to town, and that I was looking forward to their company and seeing their new abode. Then I talked briefly with Walker, and ordered room service—surf & turf and a couple of bottles of wine. I sat back in my lovely suite, and enjoyed the evening eating, drinking, and watching movies on demand.

After breakfast in my room the next morning, I went for an early morning swim, and got a quick workout in the hotel gym. *I've always loved working out, and staying in shape as best I could.* Then off to the room to get ready for what I was expecting to be a wonderful day with old friends and new acquaintances. Ryrie and Don were celebrating their 25th wedding anniversary, and had come a long way since the days we all lived in the apartment complex so many years ago. I was disappointed that Walker hadn't come, but knowing him as the jackass he was, it all make sense.

A huge, red-brick two-story mini-palace, my friends' home was gorgeous! I was so proud and happy for them, and just elated to be in their presence. They were nestled up on a quiet, private hilly cul-de-sac, away from traffic and *most* of civilization.

In their large, tree-lined backyard was a huge swimming pool with a natural waterfall, and a diverse crowd of people—some of whom I knew from way back when. Waiters in tuxedos were walking around offering beverages of all sorts, and a chef was busy at the enormous bricked oven. The food smelled delectable, and I was in heaven.

I studied the burgers, steaks and chicken on the grill, and was thinking along the lines of a rib-eye, medium-well, with a side of potato salad. *It would go well with my white wine.* I mingled, laughed with others, and met my new best friend—Kirk, the bartender. *He made for some great conversation!*

"Marley, get your swimsuit and jump in! Water's great!", someone yelled. Ryrie was laughing, just as someone pushed her head in the water. Everyone was having a good time.

I figured this would be a great time to swim—*before* the thick, juicy steak and whatever else I wanted to sink my teeth in to. "I'll just go grab my stuff," I replied as I headed toward house to get my keys out of my purse; my "stuff" was in my car, parked in front of the house.

As I walked out the front door and headed toward my car, I smiled, and thought *what a fantastic day...*I never made it back to the party.

CHAPTER 37

"MA'AM…EXCUSE ME, MA'AM…"

"Just a second….". I was reaching for my bag of swim things in the backseat of the car. I was in the front seat—driver's seat—of the car.

Beach bag in my hand, I turned around to find a police officer, staring down at me.

"Ma'am…get out of the car, please."

"Excuse me? Have I done something wrong?" I had absolutely no idea why he was questioning me. Did he want to know what was going on at this house?

"Get out of the car, Ma'am. Have you been drinking?" He was being a trite persistent. He then told me I needed to do a field sobriety test; I didn't know *what the hell* was going on. Then, he proceeded to tell me someone had called the police, complaining about the noise at the "neighborhood party". He said the caller explained there were cars blocking others' drives; mine was parked directly in front of Ryrie's house. I was blocking no one. My car hadn't moved since I'd gotten there.

I explained to this guy that I had been there a while, and just came to my car to get some items from the back seat. I wasn't going anywhere, and had actually told Ryrie and Don that I'd stay with them, if I had anything to "drink" at the party. That was my plan. But plans were made to be changed, I've always heard.

Because the temperature was outrageous, I rolled down my windows to get ventilation in the car; my key was in the ignition—had to be to power the windows. *The key was in the ignition.*

The car was on a public street, and I was in the car—the driver's seat. I never touched the wheel, nor engaged the car in any way. (Later, during court, the officer even attested to that). ...and I had been drinking. *Damnit! Damnit! Damnit!* I was arrested, for what, I wasn't sure.

Could it be? No...could it? Walker knew where I was going, yet refused to go with me. And he was jealous of every one I ever knew...even jealous of the air I breathed. And Richard, well, "The Dick"—he would go to any lengths to hurt me, no matter what the consequences. These two bastards, although they hated each other, they would conspire in any way possible to get what they wanted. Dick wanted revenge—constant revenge. Walker wanted me—for his very own, to be dependent on him. Would they, could they be so perverse, so deranged, so wicked and satanic, and so mangle-minded as to set me up? Or was this some freakish, off-the-wall, unfortunate happening—once again, in my chaotic life? It didn't matter now; I was in trouble, once again.

My lawyer-buddy of old had become an airline pilot; go figure. But he referred me to Alice—a lawyer he knew could help me in the best way—a recovering alcoholic. Someone who knew the horrors of addiction, and the legalities of its pitfalls. Alice was glad to take my case; I was just beside myself—disgusted, discouraged, and depressed.

CHAPTER 38

ALICE WAS KIND, BUT VERY tough; very thorough. I had to take her to the scene-of-the-crime—what crime, I didn't know. "We" didn't know. I re-enacted that good-day-turned-dreadful. They were trying to charge me with a DWI; we were trying to prevent it.

"Get involved in AA, and don't get out", Alice told me. "And get a sponsor." She had one; was one and sober for eleven years now. She was all-to-familiar with the hangovers, the blackouts, and the embarrassing episodes that come with being and addict—an active addict. She was also familiar with illicit affairs, and life-changing events, both good and bad. She would end up working many months, even years, and very hard to help me; she was also being paid very well.

By mid-summer, Walker and I had been through so much hell in less than two years of marriage, that we no longer felt emotions, nor had any thoughts of our own. For me, I had fallen off the ledge of "rock bottom", sinking further into a life that was fucking dead. I hated him; I hated me—everything past and present. And the future? There wasn't one. But I was still a mother, a daughter, a sister and a friend; I didn't care about the wife part—it was just "there".

The kids came home for summer vacation, and we—Sissy, Mom, Bubba and our kids—decided we all needed a well-deserved vacation. So, we packed our bags and headed where the ships sailed; we were going on a cruise. Walker couldn't go; he needed to work—good! But he kept changing his mind, over and over, until he eventually decided he'd just take us to the embarking dock. I guess he needed to make sure I was going where I said I was going, and not with some "Prince Charming" hiding behind large suitcases or cargo boxes.

Bubba began scouting the female scene, long before we boarded. He needed to know the possibilities of new "friendships", I suppose. And as I was waving a "good riddance good-bye" to Walker, I heard Bubba say with a sort of disgusted voice, "Dude, that's my sister!" *Huh?*

I turned around to find our long-time family friend—standing next to Bubba—, staring right at my ass—the cute little ass in the cuffed light-blue denim shorts. *Ok, so I'm bragging.*

Jacob Marx—Maurice's best buddy. Always there to lend a hand to Maurice, Sissy, and anyone else around that needed it. Jacob had come to help us unload, and see us off. I met him at Sissy's wedding—the second one—years ago. He had become a family friend and hunting buddy to Daddy and Bubba. When Maurice needed a right-hand-man, Jacob was always there to help out; always dependable, and very pleasant to be around. He was that kind of guy, and easy on the eyes, as well. Jacob—Jake—always showed up at bar-be-cues and various family happenings of Sissy's, so I knew him personally, somewhat. When he'd hear any of us were visiting Sissy and Maurice, he'd usually show up to have a few beers, and check out what's new from Bridgeton.

I remember when he divorced his first wife, then I'd heard he was dating someone. Shortly thereafter, Sissy told me he was getting married. For some odd reason, as I sat in her kitchen that day—so long ago—I remember thinking about him. *That was very strange.*

~✝~

For seven glorious days and nights, we sailed the ocean blue; just me and my brood—all the people I loved most in the world, minus Daddy. We swam with the dolphins, shopped the markets at various ports-of-call, saw exciting shows and enjoyed our time together.

~✝~

I had been modeling throughout the year, doing more newspapers ads and fashion shows for an old friend who owned a new women's boutique. Back on the cat-walk and enjoying every minute of it. At least I was occupying my time, and earning some extra money; I'd need it. I was about to move out, for the last time.

Walker and I finally decided enough was enough. We absolutely could not make our so-called "marriage" work. *We were done; stick a fork in us.* When I filed, I was living in the guest house once again. Preparing to move, I was all too excited about *finally* getting out of a "bad situation gotten worse".

The day I moved out, Walker asked me to go out to dinner with him. He wanted to talk over specifics of the divorce, and was feeling sort of "lonely", or so he said. I really didn't care how he felt, but I needed to eat, and a free meal sounded pretty good. We met at the restaurant where we had our first date.

"This is the last time we'll ever go out, Walker," I insisted, blatantly.

"Oh, you think so?" He questioned me, with his asinine, pretentious smart-Alek smirk.

"Oh, I know so." After that, I told him to take me home.

I didn't talk to him for several days. I was settling into my new, unsettled life, and had a photo shoot coming up for a newspaper ad I had scheduled after work one day. The shoot was to be at the river near a local park; it was for a line of clothes of a nearby department store. Mom told me she wanted to ride along.

"What do you want, Walker? You've been calling me all day, and I'm busy." I was definitely perturbed.

"I know you have the shoot, and I just wanted to wish you good luck. I love you, Marley." His voice was sad, somber. *Jeez!*

"Thanks." And I hung up.

One hour later, Walker was dead.

CHAPTER 39

WHILE I WAS STRIKING POSES with poise and charm, smiling for the camera, Walker had lost control of his new motorcycle—the "Hawg". I told him not to buy it. With our divorce coming up, he decided to trade in our trike, for this two-wheeled bike. I told him I was no longer his riding partner—or any partner for that matter—and he apparently wanted a new beginning. I said to him, "You're going to die on that thing…", and I'm sure he did it to spite me.

He was going around the curve of a country road, and lost control. The maneuverability of the new bike was so different, that he couldn't gain control after the turn. He went head-first into a concrete culvert; head first into death.

I was at Mom and Dad's when I got the news, shortly after the photo-shoot. Bubba and his fiancé, Catalina were going to meet us there. She was beautiful, and smart; they eventually broke up for some *unfortunate* reason. We were all going out to eat. Bubba came in, and told Daddy the news. Then, Daddy looked at me, and said, "Walker's dead." He explained to me what happened.

Mom looked up toward the sky, and said, "You took the wrong one…"

I looked at her, and said, "Yeah, but it's a good start."

Some speculated suicide, but I didn't. With the arsenal of weapons Walker owned, I figured a good shot right through the head would have been a better way to go. But, nevertheless, I was a widow, and my life was about to take yet *another,* unforeseen turn.

~†~

Still legally married at the time of his death, I moved back into the big house. Sure, I was upset; I wouldn't wish that on anyone, *not really.* But, as he always used to say after reading the obituaries, "Life goes on..." Yes, Walker...life goes on.

I pretty much stayed loaded for days after that, make that weeks— smoking pot, drinking heavily, and popping pills. People must have thought *I* had died. The phones were ringing constantly; uninvited people I didn't know, calling to stake their claim on whatever it was they said was theirs. At one point, I had to close and lock the front gate. People were coming down the drive, knocking on the front door, wanting to buy certain things from me—the horse trailer, the boat, the camper. One guy even came over and said he'd take the horses as payment from what Walker owed him. *WHAT!* And I know there were items missing that I swore were there before Walker died.

Then I had to decide what to do with his body. To cremate or to bury? That was the question. He had mentioned cremation to me once before during a conversation, and that's all I knew of his last wishes. So, I had him cremated. It was cheaper, and besides, it made for a great send-off party to where I was certain he'd be spending a perditions' eternity.

Lawyers were all over and everywhere. I was totally overwhelmed by what was the beginning of a long-term financial headache, although I knew it would all be to my benefit in the end. But I needed a break; to get away from the convocation of such self-serving, contentious dolts.

The pills and booze were living up to their intentions, but I needed to get out of the house and off the ranch. I had to get away from the telephones and media warfare rants regarding Walker's business and private affairs—about which I knew nothing, but to which I was now the sole heir. I was sick of the country air around me; I wanted the ocean air, the sea breeze. So, I decided to go to the Coastal Bay, and visit Sissy and her family.

PART III:

CHAPTER 40

EXACTLY ONE MONTH TO THE day of Walker's death; it would have been our two-year wedding anniversary, even if we did let the divorce go through. I arrived at Sissy's in Coastal Bay—it was a gorgeous winter's day, fresh air blowing off the coast; the sun's warmth kissing my cheeks and light, delicate skin.

The beach wasn't too crowded with off-season tourists, but with people like me escaping the realities of life on a lovely day when the coastal breeze was pleasant, crisp, and just a little salty. A cool, beautiful atmosphere and scenery.

Shortly after I arrived and had time to visit with Sissy and the kids, Maurice came in from the day at the club; I received my usual hug and "Hello, Marley…welcome!" Then came a grin; the kind you get when someone knows something about you that you're not sure you know, or not.

"What's that look for?" I asked. *Was I about to get a prize for being the 100th visitor of the week, or what? Was this FINALLY my lucky day? God, I hoped so!* I wondered, but he wouldn't tell.

"Someone's coming over to see you, Marley. I just invited him, and he'll be here any minute." *What the fuck?! I wasn't really in the mood for any more company than I'd come to see. I drove all this way to get AWAY from people!*

All of a sudden, the door opened as the doorbell rang, and in walked a tall, handsome man with pearly whites presenting a smile as big as

Texas. Although I hadn't seen him in a very long while, I knew the moustache on that smile, on that face. Jake. Jacob Marx.

Jake waltzed over to me as if I was the only person in the room; he threw his tanned, strong arms around me and hugged me as if he would never let me go. I wanted to linger in his strong, masculine embrace, but I forced myself away—I sure didn't need to be attracted to *any* man, and damn sure didn't want to!

"I wanted to call you when I heard about your husband, Walker, wasn't it? I remember him from the pier. I'm sorry about what happened. But it's good to see you, Marley…you look wonderful." And he stared at me for what seemed like an hour.

But, I stared back; our eyes were locked. *Well, except the part where I scanned his muscular chest, thick biceps and sexy, sexy mouth! What a dazzling smile—how could anyone forget that?! Better looking than I remember…hmm.*

We all sat down to a nice visit. Jake filled me in on his latest divorce, and being one of the most personable, jovial and outgoing persons I'd ever met, he kept us laughing about one thing and then another. *It was nice to laugh.* I was sure Maurice and Sissy had asked him to dine with us, but when Jake asked *me* to go out to dinner with *him,* I looked over at Maurice's approving smile, then Sissy's "Sure…she'd love to!" They practically pushed us out the door.

We ended up having a late-night bite; first, we drove to the beach, watched the sunset and smoked a fat joint. *He remembered*; Bubba and I drove over to his home once—long ago—and smoked a little weed together that day. Jake told me he had reminisced about that day many times since then; he even told me what I had been wearing! We talked, and laughed, and talked and laughed. It was wonderful. Then we dined on calamari, oysters-on-the-half-shell, and beer and wine. It was happy hour, and truly it was.

Back at his apartment by the sea, we sat on his deck and watched the cargo ships passing through the night, under the star-kissed sky. We were drinking, smoking, laughing. I remember having to go in to potty. While I was sitting on the toilet, Jake just waltzed into the bathroom, as if we'd been married for years, and began brushing his teeth.

"Uh, excuse me!" I said. Then he walked over to me, bent down, smiled and kissed my forehead. *Wow! No privacy here.* We became comfortable with each other very quickly. Then came the intimacy.

I'll never forget standing in the living room of his spacious, brightly-colored apartment. It was decorated like the inside of an aquarium—beautiful hints of blues and an array of sea life statues and ocean nostalgia, standing, hanging everywhere. I turned around to ask him a question, and there he was—in my space. His mouth was all over mine; I had no choice but to kiss him back. He told me later he had to "grab it while I could…". He didn't want to lose his nerve, or be rejected.

We engaged in some really fun necking, but it soon came time for me to leave. He had to be at work in a few hours, and I had obligations, as well. After walking me to the door in the wee morning hours, he told me he'd call me later. As much as I wanted him to, I didn't. No way in hell did I need—nor want—to jump in the waters of love, romance, or even lust—*at least never again, in this lifetime.*

My little "break" hadn't gone according to plan, but then, when in my life *had* anything gone according to my plans? I was loading my car with all the extra goodies Sissy always sent me home with—unused make-up, clothes accompanied by price tags, boxes of jewelry—things she passed along to me, as she did all through life. *Sissy was a non-stop shopper, and always had a bountiful of surprises packed up and waiting for me.*

"Your boyfriend's on the phone. He wants you to call him before you leave town." *Shit.* I hugged her and the kiddos, got in my car, and headed out faster than planned—*see, there I go again.* I was NOT going to embark on another relationship—of any kind. I liked Jacob; I truly did. But I needed to leave it at that…and just *leave.* My cell phone rang. *Again…shit!* He was such a good family friend, and I felt obligated to thank him for such a lovely time. I needed to tell him "good-bye". I also knew that unless Sissy and Maurice got divorced soon, I'd see him again someday, probably sooner than later. I answered it.

"Marley! Thank God, I caught you before you left." *Oh boy.*

"What? …You have the day off? I'm getting on the highway…what happened?" *I should NOT have answered this phone.*

"Something about the contract we were supposed to start today... boss says it's delayed until tomorrow, so he gave me the day off. This is incredible! It's never happened; the Divine plan, Marley. Please come spend the day with me. Don't go back today. Please." *Ah, man.*

Two days later: "Seriously, Jake, I have to go this time." *I guess I wasn't too persistent.*

We holed up in his apartment for what seemed like weeks—laughing, drinking, smoking, making love...*all sorts of love.* And over, and over again. We went out a couple of times to walk the beach, letting the waves tickle our toes with the sand. And then, it happened.

We were watching a movie—I introduced Jake to movies—he wasn't a movie-fanatic until he met me, or we "hooked up", I should say. Sitting shoulder-to-shoulder, up against the pillows on the bed, I saw him in my peripheral vision. He looked up at me, and I heard, "I love you." *Holy shit! Did I just hear him right?!*

I turned my head so quickly, I almost got whiplash. "What did you just say?" We both looked at each other as if we'd turned to dinosaurs. He looked as surprised as I felt. I'm not quite sure *he* knew what he had just said. We were buzzed, but we weren't wasted!

"I said I love you, Marley. I really love you."

One month later, we flew to Las Vegas and eloped.

CHAPTER 41

"BYE DADDY...HAVE A GREAT WEEKEND. Love you!" I kissed him good-bye before heading out from work. No one knew Jacob and I would be married in less than 24 hours.

"You and Jake have big plans for the weekend, honey?" Daddy knew Jake, and liked him greatly. They'd hunted many times together over the years, and got along fine. He also knew I was spending *most* of my weekends with Jake.

"Yes Sir...going to meet up in Houston...take it from there. Bye now!" I wasn't lying, nor was I expanding on the truth. I would be returning as *Mrs. Jacob Marx,* unbeknownst to everyone we knew.

Jake and I met at the airport. We were scheduled to take the red-eye to Vegas; it was on a Friday night. I had made complete arrangements—hotel, wedding plans which included limo to and from the chapel, photographer, even the kind and the color of the flowers. It was all in a wedding package. We were elated!

We waited in the airport bar, of course, toasting to each other several times. Then Jake did what was totally illegal in the airports—he lit a cigarette! All of a sudden, we're being bombarded by airport security, totally unaware of what was going on.

The guys in the three-piece suits were trying to arrest us; I just wanted to hide behind the big fichus tree next to the bar. But we begged and pleaded that it was all a simple mistake. We explained to them our excitement about being married in a few hours, and totally forgot about our surroundings, and its rules. *Jesus Christ, I was scared of being in trouble again!* We got out of that one; *Thank you, Jesus!* I was shaking as we giggled all the way to our seats on the plane.

"Ma'am, if you don't quieten down, we're going to have to land the plane, and you'll be getting off." The stewardess was a true downer. Here it was, Friday night and on the way to *Las Vegas, for crying out loud.* People were sleeping, and this bitch was being a total party-pooper. Jake and I drank and laughed all the way from Houston to Vegas…well, except for the times this "airplane waitress" threatened to throw us off the plane at thirty-thousand feet, or whatever she was saying. I stifled myself; I knew there was the possibility of me going to jail soon, just didn't want it to be tonight.

We spent the wee morning hours getting our wedding license, then caught a few hours of shut-eye before heading out to be married. First, though, we went downstairs to take a dip in the beautiful, multi-level pool, and enjoyed cocktails at the underwater bar.

Our wedding was gorgeous; *we* were gorgeous! Elvis Chapel was lovely—a tiny little white clapboard, old house-turned-chapel, complete with Reverend and his wife—photographer and witness. Lavender orchids were everywhere; it was like a spring meadow full of flowers. We said our "I do's" and rode the limo back to our beautiful honeymoon suite. After Jake carried me over the threshold, I thought we'd entered heaven. What I saw next was the most romantic scene my eyes had ever witnessed.

"Oh Jake! It's beautiful! This is why I waited for you so long in the limousine. You didn't forget the rings. You did this…*all of it!!*" I had tears in my eyes as they scanned the entire suite, complete with beautifully-lit scented candles, and rose petals everywhere. And I mean, *everywhere!!* I never wanted to leave this room, and especially this man.

We drank champagne, toasting to the new "Mr. and Mrs. Marx", and consummated our matrimonial union. We were so much in love. Then we jetted down to the casinos, played some slots; Jake tried his hand at blackjack and some other stuff. I was enjoying the free wine; he the beer. We strolled all through the streets, in awe of the amazing light shows and fantastic atmosphere.

By midnight, we were atop the Stratosphere, riding the thrill rides at over 110 stories high.

"No one, and I mean NO ONE, could EVER get me to do this, except you, Marley!" I was laughing so hard at Jake that my stomach hurt! He was laughing at my hair being blown straight over my head; told me I looked like one of those old-fashioned cupie-dolls. Bless his heart; he hated roller coasters and thrill rides, and here he was doing all this stuff for me. *Wow, what a man!* But, I witnessed him having more fun at fifty, than he'd ever had in his life; and he was more in love than he'd ever been with anyone, even me. *Maybe, I thought, this can be a new trend. I have always loved thrill rides!*

We walked back to our hotel. People yelled at us; "woo-hoo!" they hollered. I could have sworn we had "Just Married" written all over our asses. But then, poor Jakey confessed to me that he had "the thing" on his head—*in* his head. He told me he had the worst headache imaginable, so we went up to the room, I gave him some aspirin, and he went to sleep. *Poor guy. The price one pays for love.* I was still laughing.

A few short hours, the sun came up. Jake felt a little better, but still had "the thing". I gave him more aspirin, and ordered room service—Spanish omelet and champagne for me; English muffin and bloody Mary's for him. Then, casually, we strolled down to the casino and sat at the bar while waiting for our cab. We hopped on a plane, and headed back to Texas.

CHAPTER 42

WE WERE INSANE, BUT MADLY in-love. Living almost three-hundred miles apart; his life on the coast, mine in the country—we were now married. And we had no plan, whatsoever. *I've realized as life goes by, when I don't have a plan, that's when it turns out the best.*

I disclosed—at the very beginning of our tiny courtship—my entire life's story to Jacob—at least the shitty party about the trouble I was in and the chaos around me. I told him I had no idea what to expect or where I'd be in the coming months, years; he didn't care one way or another.

"You need to turn and run like hell from me, as fast as you can go." I demanded. "You don't want to be anywhere close to my life right now, Jake. Do yourself a favor, and leave me be." I tried to tell him; tried to warn him. But my honesty and humility only drew him closer.

"You're one hell of a good woman, Marley. And you're willing to risk your happiness by saving mine. Most women would tie a man around their finger, *then* reel him in and unload their baggage. But you're different…and I love you for that." *Jesus…that wasn't what I intended.* And now, we were one, though miles and miles apart.

That was one of the most fun years of my entire life. For almost ten months, we spent every weekend commuting back and forth, satisfying our desirous appetites for love, lust, and everything in between. One weekend the beach, the other in the country. Back and forth, we knew but one destination—each other.

He taught me to gig crab and deep-sea fish; I taught him to saddle-up and ride horses. Every moment together was a new and exciting adventure—every second together we were falling deeper in love. We ate and drank like King Henry and his favorite wife! And we *never* lacked for laughter and love. The world was ours, and we were the only two people in it.

Most weekends were extended, and often during the week our yearning for each other demanded we rendezvous mid-way. We would always meet at the same hotel—usually the same room. When our eyes met, laughter began, as did life. I couldn't stop my car fast enough to get out and run to his open arms, and that large dooly he drove, well, I was sure somebody would get hurt being in the way.

We would have our usual spirits, eat out at one of our favorite restaurants, and go back to the room and laugh, love, and stay up as late as we could. Neither one of us wanted to lose a single minute sleeping—our time together was too precious.

And the very few times throughout the first year, when we weren't together, we were on the phone hours on end, laughing, over and over, and over. But then the time came for us to make a decision. Someone needed to move.

With all the indignation of my legal problems, we decided it best that Jacob move to Bridgeton. Actually, that was the only sensible thing to do. So, we loaded up my island-boy—my husband and best friend—and moved him to the country.

Setting up house as husband and wife was easy, and we were having a blast. But I could have lived under a bridge in a cardboard box and been none-the-wiser, as long as I was with Jake. We were exploring our new love, and new life—together.

CHAPTER 43

OUR FIRST FULL WINTER TOGETHER, and we decided to take a road trip. We both loved snow-skiing, but had never done it together. So, we thought we'd try our luck on the slopes.

The log cabin was sweet and quaint—perched up on the side of a snow-topped hill on the outskirts of Ruidoso; we kept the fireplace lit. I serenaded Jake with screeching strums of the guitar I'd brought along—that was the sound it made when I *tried* to play it. I knew nothing about playing a guitar. But, I thought it romantic, and dragged it along.

We ate, drank and smoked dope like it was our last good time on earth; all to the tune of freedom, love, happiness and new adventures.

Our first day on the slopes, Jake's ski fell off as we rode the lift to the summit of the mountain. I grabbed him; he was about jump for it.

"What the hell!? You can't jump. You'll break your legs!" I couldn't believe he'd actually jump that far down for a stupid ski.

"I've got to go after it." He said. "What am I supposed to do, slalom off?"

"Well, yeah…that's your only choice." *Seriously!?* He reached for my arm, as if to hold on to it for some odd reason.

I quickly put his hand back on his person. "No way, dude. You're not taking me down with you. No sense in *both* of us going down!" I explained to him that Bubba and Sissy and I had made a rule long ago; if you know you're going to eat snow, you do it alone. No sense in taking anyone else with you.

"Marley! Are you kidding me? You're not going to help me?" We were approaching the unloading dock.

As I gracefully skied off and down the exit ramp, I turned only to find Jake hobbling—two legs on one ski—plummeting nose-first into the snow. I began an act of laughter that I swear created an avalanche! I was laughing so hard I couldn't see straight! Jake was a mess, bless his heart.

Then we both looked over at the "Three Amigos" perched atop the side of a hill. They were resort workers, taking a break. I swear they were all bent over, laughing harder than me.

"Dude, we're not laughing at you," one of them insisted as he pointed to me. "We're laughing at her, laughing at you!" I laughed even harder; did so for days and days.

While blowing snow out of his facial orifices, Jake removed his one ski and began trudging downslope. "Fuck it!" he said. "Let's go to the bar." So, we did.

We didn't ski much after that. But we drove around sight-seeing; taking in the beautiful snow-drenched mountains and flowing, clear springs of the valleys. No postcard in the world could ever exhibit a more serene, lovely site!

When we returned home, we got the dreaded news; I had a court hearing coming up. After almost three years of postponed court dates, the one that would finally determine my fate and freedom—or lack thereof—was just around the corner. But we weren't afraid; we weren't worried. We had each other, until death do us part, regardless of whether or not we'd be forced to be apart for any determined length of time. From the beaches to the mountains, we were taking in every precious moment that presented the opportunity. Money was no object, and we were living like it was our last hurrah. And it was, for a while.

CHAPTER 44

THE OFFER OF SEVEN YEARS became five, which became three; or ten years of probation.

"Remember, Marley, this is your second felony. Three years is as low as they'll go, or you can do the ten years on probation", explained my high-powered, very highly-paid lawyer. "And if you do the probation, you'll have to enter into a rehabilitation program, within the judicial system. It's a boot-camp-type rehab. You'll be wearing white like everyone else in the prison system, and you'll be incarcerated, but you won't be 'in prison', so they tell me. Then you'll do nine years' probation, after that." *This was NOT what I wanted to hear.* And so, it was.

Alice explained to me that it's taken almost three years because "they" —the team of national lawyers working on this case—could not find *what to do* in my particular situation. Although I never touched the wheel of the car, thus the vehicle never moved, but the *key was in the ignition.* Because of this, I was charged a DWI; because I had priors. She also explained that it could have been dropped, or at least degraded to a misdemeanor, had I not possessed such a history of alcohol-related arrests.

"I'll take the ten years." Actually, I felt relieved. No way was I going to go to "prison".

~†~

The nearly-five months spent in county jail was horrific. I had never been treated like such a second-class citizen than during this time. But, even in jail I was offered an "honorary position" —that of trustee. Dark blue looked way better on me than stripes, anyway. I did my time with grace in my soul, kept to myself, and didn't make waves.

Often times someone would say something like, "You don't look like you belong here…" No, I don't, but I am.

"Addiction has no biases; it has no favorites," I'd reply. Very basic, but difficult for many to understand.

I attended Catholic Mass every week, and prayed constantly for strength, peace, and hope; not only for myself, but my family at home and the ladies with whom I was incarcerated. I read one book after another, usually a romantic novel, or something comedic; anything that would take me away—get my mind off of reality. Then one day, my name was called.

Hand-cuffed and shackled, I arrived at the place I'd live for the next six, maybe seven months. The "boot-camp-rehab" was vicious, vile, and wicked. It was the worst thing I'd ever imagined, and more; literally, an army in white. But, I kept my head up, attended the counseling sessions daily, and did the best I could with what I had to work with. I did whatever I was told to do; I was determined NOT to make matters worse—if that was possible—by rebelling in any way. I took classes of various sorts to pass the time and improve whatever it was I could improve, and even had the job of school tutor. *It sure beat the hell out of being on the hoe squad! I did that at the beginning. No way in hell could I have maintained that for six months!* I was grateful for the "privileged", air-conditioned job.

The program was strict with a no-nonsense policy. These people were ferocious, and I wasn't laughing. It was tough—scary tough. Although there were many upper-class, educated women like myself, there were low-life, uncivilized idiots who seemed to prey on stupidity. That was one of the hardest things about being there; having to live amongst losers with no morals or standards of any sort, obviously raised in the wild by loser-ancestors.

But with my job as tutor, I was able to help some who helped themselves, and that made my time vaguely tolerable. And on the weekends,

Jake and the kids came to visit; Jake never missed one weekend in over a year, coming to see me. Sometimes Mom and Dad would visit as well. We couldn't talk on the phone; there were no phone visits, so I got letters from the family regularly. Jake and I wrote each other almost daily. *I think I felt more loved by Jake, than ever before. I was blessed—truly blessed.*

I had nightmares for months after I got home, but at least I was home. I'd never smelled anything so good as the sweet smell of freedom swirling around me the day I left that hell. Never again did I want to drink. I hadn't had a drop of alcohol for over a year, and with nine years of "supervision" headed my way, no way in hell was I about to look back at the torture from where I'd just come. After what I'd just gone through, I knew I could do anything. I was on a mission—from here on out—to do things the right way, soberly.

CHAPTER 45

JAKE AND I WERE ON top of the world, once again. He took a few weeks off work to spend time with me, and we laid around in our pajamas for days—loving, laughing, watching movies. We watched the news of Hurricane Katrina; such devastation. I felt so lucky, so fortunate to be where I was, and with Jake. We made some donations, said many prayers, and were happy to be starting over—sober, free, and in love.

While I was locked away in treatment, Jake was working on his own sobriety. He'd pledged to stop drinking; couldn't smoke dope anymore due to random testing at work, so we were dedicated to living a very healthy lifestyle—*for a while, anyway.*

Time moved on, and so did we. During the winters, we snow-skied; summers we spent at the beach—fishing, surfing, all the fun things we loved to do together. We took mini-cruises throughout the year, and enjoyed camping at various state parks during cooler times. Drove to the Grand Canyon one spring where we hiked 'til we could walk no more. I was attending meetings when I could get to them, and even began to take some college courses. Life was going good, and we were doing great.

We absolutely adored the holidays. Spending time with family was important to us, and we usually took our annual mountain-trip to a ski resort we had yet to visit, around this time; that was typically our Christmas gift to each other.

I loved to decorate the house festively—for whatever occasion time brought. But the holiday season was special; it was a time for giving, and appreciating the blessings bestowed upon us by God. We were always grateful, and we tried to live accordingly. This year would be no different...*but it was.*

Weather was cool; brisk wintery breezes blowing in happiness from all over. The world around us lit up with holiday lights of bright Christmas colors, people smiling merrily while wishing each other the best of the holiday season. Santas on every corner ringing their bells for those less fortunate. *I always liked to empty my wallet of any pocket change, and stuff a few dollar bills in the kettle if I could.*

'Tis the season for holiday cheer, and I'm not just talking about attitudes. All over and everywhere people were toasting to good times, old acquaintances and new friends. What was a Christmas morning without Bailey's in my coffee? How could I hostess a holiday open-house and show off my festively decorated home without a punchbowl full of eggnog—*spiked eggnog, that is.* And for the first time in a few years, I really wanted to ring in the new year with a glass of champagne. So, that's what we did.

"You'll be fine, Marley. Just this once..." he'd say.

"I can just have some champagne, just this time..." I'd say. We searched for ways to justify our desires. We tried, and tried, and were strongly successful for a while. But finally, we succumbed. And there I was, back in the saddle, again. *Or should I say, "off the wagon", again.* And, so was Jake.

For a while it was a couple of beers for him, a bottle of champagne for me. But, soon the champagne didn't fulfill the euphoria I was seeking, and one bottle turned in to two. By now I figured, *what the hell?* I might as well drink the wine I so craved—it was cheaper, and it was, if I would have just kept it at one. And to keep up with me, Jake was drinking more, as well.

~✝~

We started out having fun, but things didn't always end up that way. There were mornings I'd wake to find a very strange look in Jake's eyes—a look that told me something was wrong. I didn't like the things he told me that went on the night before, and I usually ended up expressing an apology—about things I didn't recall.

"Oh Jake, honey, there's no way I'd ever say those things to you! I'm so sorry." I felt like a heel. A real piece of shit.

"Come here, Marley. Give me a hug and tell me you'll never say those things again. Tell me you love me." My apologies were always genuine; they just didn't seem to last.

Often, I promised not to drink that day—after being a bitch to the man I adored. The things I did and said in a drunken stooper were inexcusable, and they weren't "me". I would never in my right mind do some of the things I did—throw my most precious items across the room, or curse Jake like a maniacal tyrant. But that's just it—I *wasn't* in my right mind. I was drunk, blacked out, a sot.

But we'd go to the store; Jake would bring home some beer and buy some wine for me. "Just don't drink it all…" or "Drink it slower this time…" He was always trying to make me feel better for what I'd done the night before. Pour me a drink to help me forget. So, here we'd go, again.

But things didn't *always* turn our horrible when we'd drink. Thing is, I never knew if it would, or not. I tried to drink responsibly, but somehow the wine caught up with me, and I'd black out. Do stupid shit, or not. It was all the toss of a coin, and no heads or tails could ever predict the outcome. If we'd had a gypsy fortune teller, she couldn't have predicted how our evenings would end up. I guess you could say Jake and I always "hoped for the best". It usually turned out for the worst.

CHAPTER 46

COMMUNITY SERVICE WAS A BITCH! Hundreds and hundreds of hours I spent working for somebody else—for free, in addition to my full-time job. I hated every minute of it, and it took me several years to complete. *I like volunteering, but this was ridiculous!* Besides, this wasn't what I would have chosen to do, if I were volunteering.

But, as soon as I'd arrive home, I'd go straight to the fridge where a nice, cool glass of white wine awaited. *Ah, the fruits of my labor!* Jake was a sweetheart, and he knew how hard I was working. He was my love, my best friend…my enabler. He was co-dependent on me, and we were a team of two, on a mission—to self-destruct.

With the kids getting older and in the "city that never sleeps", they weren't coming around much. Oh sure, Jake and I would travel to see them in their ball games, school plays, and spend our time with them whenever possible, but they were growing up; not wanting parents breathing down their necks in all things they did. And they hated the country; hated it. So, we were seeing less of them as time went by. It was sad, but so be it. Had Dick not been such a "dick", I'm sure things would have been much more pleasant. But we absolutely did not get along—he wouldn't let it happen—so Jake and I had sporadic happenings with the young ones. They adored Jake and loved me dearly, but things were changing; as Walker always said, "…life goes on". I think this contributed greatly to the increase in my elbow exercises. I think it did for both of us—Jake, and me.

The probation era was going all right, I guess. A major inconvenience, but I was pretty much doing what I was supposed to. Well, no, not really. I was drinking, and not supposed to be. But after so many years, it seems my P.O. moved on to bigger and more serious cases. Although I'd had some close calls, all was going pretty well. I was taking advantage of the situation, though, and living on the edge of a double-edged sword. I was seriously pressing my luck, and barely getting by—but getting by.

Work was going great, however. When I completed my community service tenure, I began volunteering for the less fortunate population of my community. I loved it, and I had the time to give the compassion of my heart. With no kids around and work slowing down, I decided I needed to do something to help others, and "give back", so to speak. My "giving back" lead to a great career change—a true calling.

Grandma Thomson had been very ill, and we went to visit her for the last time—God rest her soul. This lead to my "calling". I saw how people in the nursing home treated her with love—the kind of love they'd give to their own grandmother—and I wanted to be a part of it all. I knew from that day forward, I wanted to work with the elderly, the sick and the dying.

I've often thought of using the excuse that working in such a depressing, often sad environment caused me to drink so. But, that wasn't the case. I drank if I was sad or happy, whether it was raining or sunny.

I remember coming back to Texas on the early morning flight. The stewardess asked if one of us would sit up near the front in an empty seat. One of the seats we were in was needed for a disabled man. I obliged. I also sat up there, and drank three glasses of wine—*for breakfast*. It went well with the Xanax I had taken before the flight—it calmed my nerves. Never mind the addiction; it was an "additive".

~✝~

Jake and I continued on our yearly vacations—both winter, and summer—living life large and enjoying *most* of it. I was going to school year-round; it was a total challenge, but I loved learning, and loved feeling productive. Plus, it kept me sober, *somewhat*.

I was trying to spend more time at church, and Jake was picking up more hours at work. We lacked for nothing; money wasn't an object. We enjoyed country walks, riding the horses, and sitting on the patio watching the wild turkeys and the deer. Sometimes a fox would zip past our peripheral; it was a good thing we both saw it since one of us was always demanding confirmation from the other. We talked about moving, making a change in the scenery that surrounded us. But one thing would *not* change—our drinking. *And two-gun Sally would come to call.*

Jake was on my ass about something; I'm not sure what. Didn't have to be much, if we were drinking. He'd bring the booze in the house, we'd start drinking, then he'd get pissed off at me for something I said or did. This particular night, I wasn't about to hear it. That's when I decided I'd be a real live, Western bandit.

Two pistols—loaded—were within my reach; that wasn't good, considering my inebriated and frustrated state of being. Jake was a hunter, and a protective husband, but tonight he probably wished he'd have taken his chances with fate. He was thinking tonight he just might meet his destiny.

I grabbed the two pistols—one in each hand, of course. One gun was a new model, you know, the kind with a "clip". The other was an old-fashioned revolver. It had a 6-bullet barrel, and a real snazzy ivory, engraved handle. I believe I inherited it from Walker, who was its heir from years gone by. Anyway, all I needed was a holster, some boots— they were in the closet- and a ten-gallon hat—that was in the closet, as well. But I wasn't kidding, and neither was I in my right mind to know what I was doing. But, I certainly *did* know I'd never pull the trigger— not on the man I love. *Shit, I'd never shoot anybody, for that matter. No way, no how.* That was insane, and so were these moments.

Jake was across the room, and I drew both guns as if I was Two-Gun Sally in a Dodge City shootout. His eyes were as big as bowling balls, and he froze; just froze in his stance, not knowing what to do. *To move, or not to move…that was the question.* His thoughts were, *'If I move, she'll shoot me. If I don't, I'm committing suicide.'*   And he stood there, staring at me with wild, wide eyes—filled with the fear of death; I just laughed.

"I'd never hurt you, Jake..." and he stepped across the threshold as fast as he could. Then, a shot; the bullet went through the cedar door—the one Jake had only moments ago been standing in front of—after I pulled the trigger of the 6-shooter. I don't remember if I knew the damn thing was loaded, or not. I kind of thought, *'Oh shit! Uh oh!'* I was kind of playing with him that night, but kind of not.

The family members staying in our guest house never knew about the one-sided dual.

I got up early the next morning to go run a charity 5K I'd been looking forward to for quite some time. Afterward I went to eat a bite of brunch with some close acquaintances. I was still sort of pissed off—at him, and me; sort of felt ashamed. I didn't want to go home and face Jake, especially with other people around; I didn't know what the atmosphere at home would be like, and I was too tired to want to find out. When I got back in the car and checked my messages, there was one from Jake. "Baby Doll, don't forget the beer and wine on your way home; grillin' steaks for everybody tonight."

CHAPTER 47

AND THAT'S THE WAY THINGS were with us; we'd buy booze, drink, fight. Then we'd make up, buy it again, and the cycle started all over—consistently...stinkin' thinkin'—doing the same thing and expecting different results. The thing is, we sometimes had favorable outcomes, but we couldn't bank on it.

I always knew I had a drinking problem. Hiding bottles of wine in my shoes—boots were always the safest—, various corners of my closet, inside make-up kits; I'd be an imbecile to think there wasn't a problem. I once knew someone with an addiction to chocolate; she hid packages of chocolate candy bars in her dirty clothes hamper. No one would think to look in there, or would they? Only an addict—a manipulator; someone who secretly lies by omission, but never with malicious intent; the intent is just the opposite. It's meant to protect herself, and the ones she loves. It's a crazy lifestyle; a bedlam of sorts. But it's reality—*my* reality.

You can bet that a quiet weekend away with the family was a sobering event. *Well, not entirely*. One can rest assured that I had little bottles of stash hidden inside my suitcase, and I *dare* anyone to go through my personal things.

Jake—sweet, loving, precious Jake. Often our mini-trips were made with promises of sober times, usually due to occurrences from previous events. But Jake was the one usually to break down and hand me a spirit when we'd get back to the hotel from a day with the fam. I always felt like a kid being rewarded for a good deed, or perhaps getting all A's on my report card—*he always noticed*. But I'd attempt to keep my promises;

Jake enabled me to break them. The vicious cycle of addiction at its ultimate finest!

Back at home, hiding bottles underneath shrubbery made for a lovely after-dinner stroll—alone, of course—*and drink.*

And I can't count the number of times I've excused myself to use the "ladies" room, even in my own home, when entertaining. I've wondered, if anyone wondered, why my iced-tea level was never changing.

~†~

Jake had never seen a jail cell or the likes of catastrophic legal troubles, even as much as he drank and smoked over the years. Either he was that good, or that good at being lucky. I'm sure it was the latter that prevailed. Alcohol had a hold of me and it wasn't about to let go. Sure, I tried, and I'd succeed often times at being sober and staying out of trouble. But when my dopamine kicks in, my judgment takes a hiatus.

Alcohol is a progressive disease; it gets worse over time. The affects increase while the defects grow deeper. What were good times "back in the day" had become horror stories—or so I've been told—and spectacles of chaos and unwanted drama. What used to take a bottle to get me "feeling good" now took two, sometimes three. I drank wine like a kid drinks Kool-Aid after a day of playing in summer sun. Alcohol deteriorates the body, eats up brain cells and tears up the soul. And wherever I was buying it—store, restaurant, bar—I always bought the cheap shit just to be able to buy more of it. Sick. Very sick.

Often times I resented the phrase Jake would say when he was walking toward me to refill my glass, "She's got her best friend with her..." He never knew I added to his phrase, silently, *"yes, and her worst enemy".* But I liked to drink; the drink didn't always like me.

After a while, it all just became a habit with us—an unhealthy, expensive, really bad habit. Sometimes I'd realize I didn't want to consume the drink, but whether or not it was within reach often determined my mood. I wanted it to be in the fridge, or the cupboard, *just in case.*

I once figured up the amount of hard-earned cash we were wasting on booze annually. Whether purchasing it at the market or a restaurant, the amount surpassed what we were paying on property taxes; an amount that equaled two fun-filled, week-long, well-deserved and thought-out vacations per year—*for two people! Talk about a buzz-kill!*

CHAPTER 48

SO, I TRADED IN MY horses for a pool. *Oh, the things we do for true love*! Now we were in a lovey red-brick home in the suburbs—a far cry from the country atmosphere I'd lived in for many years. But, Jake was more in his element, and although I sacrificed for the guy who had my heart, we were both closer to work, grocery stores and other places in which I was involved. Besides, the memories of unhappy times with Walker and those for the kids needed to be buried—kind of like Walker's ashes were buried down by the creek in the woods, next to his departed furry friends.

We had an estate sale and sold everything; went from pure ranch-style to total contemporary. The backyard looked like a Bahamian paradise, complete with swimming pool, rock gardens and palm trees—our own private vacation spot. And being the free-spirited, immodest hippies, we were, we had 8' fences installed on all sides of the yard; we didn't want "tan lines", and didn't want to be arrested, either.

Our beautiful new home would be the beginning of an era in making wonderful memories together—the two of us and our children—whenever they decided to "come home". Jake and I were set now.

We always knew there was an amazing devotion for one another; a unique and very close relationship. One that would outlive any obstacles and bumpy roads in our paths. A love and friendship made especially for us, that would endure any problem created in this worldly life.

~†~

The first few summers were spent basking in the sun in our laps of luxury. Jake and I would plan our occasional day off or play "hooky" from work to enjoy the finer things in life—our home. Just the two of us—Jake and Marley Marx—grillin' and chillin' in the warmth of a June or July Texas sun. Usually the aroma of rib-eyes and chicken on the grill filled the summer air; sometimes jumbo shrimp and large scallops made our "surf & turf" meal just perfect. And of course, we had hits of the 60's, 70's and 80's chiming away on the backyard stereo. *Ah, life is good!*

Autumn always brought weekends by the double-sided fireplace; watching our favorite college football teams—whichever ones we had bets on for that week—on the big-screen television was always a favorite past time.

But no summer fun-days or autumn games were complete without a refrigerator full of our favorite refreshing beverages, usually beer and wine. *Now, let the games begin!*

CHAPTER 49

ONE FATHER'S DAY, AS I sat in the living room planning our winter vacation at a mountain casino resort—oh, those free-flowing spirits—Jake had an idea.

"Baby, why don't you take your Dad to Hawaii this year. He'd love to tour Pearl Harbor, and you're always telling me how proud you are of the veterans you work with. Y'all would have a blast. You can tell him later tonight when you talk to him."

I was really surprised, but Jake had never expressed a desire to go to Hawaii, and I was always bugging him to take me. So, I called Daddy, wished him "Happy Father's Day", and invited him to go to Hawaii. He was as surprised as I was, and just as excited.

Years ago, Daddy and I traveled to Florida to visit my paternal relatives; it was an aunt's and uncle's Golden Anniversary, and many of my relatives were attending. We stayed in a high-rise condo on the Western beach of Florida, and we all had a lovely time. Not much drinking there. In fact, I don't recall alcohol being a part of the party. It may have been, but certainly wasn't any big deal.

Each year my family has tried to take vacations together. Sometimes they prove to be successful, sometimes not. Whoever drinks usually ends up pissing everyone off. I used to be the scape-goat; seems like I was always the culprit until shit would go down between, say, Mom and Sissy, when I wasn't even around. Those are the times I loved to tell Daddy or Jake, "See…I'm not even there! Can't blame it on me this time!"

The year O.J. Simpson did the famous white Bronco runaway scene, I went to the East Coast with some traveling companions—very dear to me—who will remain nameless. We toured phenomenal historical sights, and experienced places most people only dream about visiting. It was wonderful—at first. We were teetotalers throughout the entire vacation; no one drank at all. But there were pills—lots of pills—being taken by one individual in particular. Stresses were high, and we could have probably benefited from having a drink at the end of the day, but that wasn't the case.

To make a long "good-story-gone-bad" short, I was left in the parking lot of a gas station, in the middle of the night, somewhere in the Appalachian fucking mountains. We were on our way home, and the stresses from the days had built up so much that the counter effects of the pills outweighed the good they were supposed to do. *It isn't true that 'more is better'.* I was left. Period. I was able to get home, after some very scary situations trying to get to safety, then home. *Addiction comes in all forms, and no one is better than the other(s)*

Back in Hawaii with Daddy, we enjoyed our 43rd, penthouse condo overlooking Waikiki Beach—it was incredible! We climbed Diamond Head, attended a Luau, and cussed out all the traffic to and from. I even got Daddy to share a celebratory glass of champagne with me the night we arrived. I know he only agreed to it with me to "keep the peace", and I appreciated his "what the hell" attitude. I enjoyed wine at the pool's bar, and on the eight-hour flight over the Pacific Ocean, but all-in-all, it turned out to be a very nice trip.

~✝~

The trip to the casino resort was grand, and so was my credit card bill that season. It was already deep autumn, and the plethora of colors on the mountain trees were all sorts of golden, rust, brown, and every-thing in between.

While Jake and his parents were winning at games of Blackjack, I was babysitting the slots and paying full-attention to the waitress. *When you tip the waitress, she keeps coming back with free glasses of wine.* She was sort of adopting me as her favorite customer and I was allowing the resort to pick up the bar tab—mine.

At one point, I knew I had ingested more wine than I should have because I insisted on leaving our puny-ass room, and had all our belong-ings moved to some huge "Safari Suite", complete with zebra-striped rugs, African-décor, a full kitchen and fireplace. It also came with a huge nightly price tag, but I knew the more I drank, the less I cared; and so, I did, and didn't.

But, we had a fun time, and I wrote the high-priced room off as balancing out with the free booze. *It all washes out in the end, or so I made myself believe.*

~†~

Ah, the coming of spring! Fresh flowers everywhere—bluebonnets all along the Texas highways; fields being used as landscapes while parents park along the feeder roads, unloading kids and pets, putting together the family portrait. Sweethearts taking selfies in fields of sun-flowers and daisies, and everyone taking in the fresh air and Vitamin D. And Jake's and my anniversary.

This particular year, I booked us a suite in a luxury hotel in the midst of a thriving, revamped, downtown Metropolis. Just a quiet four-day weekend with romantic evening walks and dinners out, maybe catch a play, do a little shopping, and a train ride through the surrounding country, or so I thought.

"Wow! What the hell's going on down here?!" I asked with surprise as we drove up to the famous, century-old hotel—it happened to be the very last place President JFK spent his last night.

"Marley, did you know all this was going on?" Jake asked, suspiciously.

Now something about Jake and me: We do NOT like crowds. The valet guy told us it was the annual, international art, food and wine festival. *How could I have missed this!? Well, so much for a quiet, romantic weekend. Or was it?*

The 36-block festival was also a 4-day event, and we had both just arrived. When it was all said and done, over half a million people had attended, and we actually had a real fun time—*what I remember of it.*

Oh sure, I found my favorite art—wine. Red wines, white wines, wines of blush and rose'. Beverage booths were almost as abundant as booths of clothes, paintings, jewelry—just about anything you can think of to decorate and sell. The event was truly fascinating, but we didn't get by without a *hitch,* naturally.

Apparently, I made a scene at the expensive steak house the first night we were there. (Did I mention our hotel also had a *free* evening happy hour for guests?) Whether I flirted with the waiter or bitched out the manager, it was a bit over-the-top, or so I was told. But, we had a nice time, with no ill-fated words—*none too serious.*

This is the kind of trip I liked to take; my Baby and me, and drinking makes three. We spaced things out, of course; we weren't just two lushes running wild in the street. *Well, Jake wasn't, anyway.*

The next day we enjoyed dance moves of all sorts; there was a different culture of music practically on every corner. We strolled through the streets and tents of abstract paintings, eccentric jewelry, and even bought some matching tie-dyed shirts. The wine was flowing in my mouth and Jake was keeping up with his elbow exercises, as well. And the day was filled with breaths of fresh air.

Back to the hotel to freshen up and regroup, then on to the concierge's happy hour for delectable appetizers and our favorite spirits—free—before heading out for the evening.

The downtown streets were all abuzz with folks from every walk of life enjoying serenades from a plethora of musical instruments. The street-lined trees were brightly lit, glistening colorfully as people strolled up one way and down another, each person enthralled in their own little consequential world. The old historical buildings seemed to come alive with the vibrant atmosphere; truly a sight to behold.

Jake and I decided Cajun food would be our delight for the evening's meal, so we waltzed our way through the busy streets and into one of the crowded restaurants. We found our seats at the hostess' chosen table, and enjoyed a delicious meal while we laughed, people-watched and took in all the festival sounds. Then, I excused myself to the ladies' room. We had just finished paying the dinner check.

~†~

"Where the hell did you go?" Jake asked me bright and early the next morning, as he came out of the bedroom. I was fixing two cappuccino's—compliments of our hotel kitchenette.

"Huh? What are you talking about?" I was totally puzzled, and not sure I wanted to be a partner in this virgin conversation. I quickly scanned the room. My clothes from last night were neatly placed over the living room chair. Purse was hanging from its usual temporary place on the arm of the dining chair. *Hmmm...* My jewelry—*Thank God!*—and hotel keycard were in their places on the living room side table.

"From the restaurant? I waited and waited, and you never came back. I looked for you at the bar, asked the waitress to look for you in the restroom. So, I walked the streets looking for you, and finally came back to the room. Kept calling your cell phone." He wasn't too happy.

Yep, the cell phone was next to the key card; three messages, all from Jake. I had no clue as to what he was talking about, so what possible explanation could I give? I was busted. But, with what? A lie? The truth? Definitely a blackout. I'm sure I made up some cock-a-Mamie story, but no doubt blamed it on the booze—twelve hours' worth. Jacob was used to it, I suppose. I guess that's why he gave up and came on back to the hotel. He knows when I'm in that "state". Although he was worried, he knows I'm a functional sot, and I'll find my way back to where I need to be. I've never been one of those side-winding, bumping-into-people falling-down-drunks. Just someone who's memory escapes me for periods of time, at random. I never intend to get to that point—it just happens at various times of intoxication. Obviously, I wasn't hurt and

I'm sure I had a good time. But like a curious child or puppy, I wondered off, went astray into my own adventure. Poor Jake.

But stranger than strange; a very odd item found its way into my purse that night. I'll just leave it at that. Certain things are better left unsaid, and unexplained. *Maybe.*

We continued to enjoy our anniversary holiday.

CHAPTER 50

SCHOOL WAS GOING FULL-FORCE. I was working to complete my Bachelor's degree and making good grades. Work was steady, and with each day on the horizon, my prayer was to help someone, in some way; I wanted to make a positive impact on someone's life before I laid my head down that night. Charity events and the volunteer work I was involved with were definitely seeing results in the lives of those we touched; I've always tried to be a part of an actively compassionate community. I was offered some truly remarkable positions that would benefit not just my career, but inspire the wellness of community neighbors in teaching them how to life a healthier lifestyle. *For some, this may sound hypocritical; to me, it was a calling. The choice of how, and when we deal with our chronic conditions and/or illnesses is our own. Often, we're better caretakers of others than we are ourselves.* And…I was a singer in a band.

Dear ol' Uncle Frank and a few of his old band members were forming a new band, and sometimes filled in for others at gigs here and there. They asked me to be their vocalist. With my love for singing, and his instrumental talents—along with his managerial expertise—we knew we were on to something that could prove to be prosperous. Music was in our blood, and we had—at different times in our lives—been dedicated musicians. (I absolutely adore music, and had also been in a couple of bands along the way, but nothing serious evolved).

We practiced and practiced, and if that's all we ever did, it would have been enough for both of us. But, before we knew it, we were playing at county fairs, community centers and area venues. I was belting out everything from Patsy Cline to Pat Benatar, feeling like a true diva and having a blast with every note.

Even at the bars where we played, I never as much as took a sip of anything other than water or a Diet Coke. I was on the most natural high. Besides, I knew that any state other than total sobriety would hinder my voice, and I expected nothing from myself other than a peak performance.

Then, abruptly, our music career ended. Uncle Frank died playing the drums, doing what he loved to do most. And he was sober doing it. He taught me so much, and for that short era in my life, I was so very proud; felt so wonderfully unique. And the queerest thing about it was that I sang at his funeral. It was an honor and a privilege, and it was the best performance I have ever given. *God rest your soul, Uncle Frank.*

I know that one option for me in the future is to be aware of places I go that can trigger my sobriety, or lack thereof. Also, people and activities are some things to consider for future outings. So often it's just as easy to step into a local meeting of "Friends of Bill W." than it is to chance messing up a good time by just taking one drink. I'll have to remember to put those meetings on my activities' agendas.

CHAPTER 51

MANY SEMESTERS OF YEAR-ROUND COLLEGE had finally paid off; I graduated with my Bachelor's Degree. Walking across the stage and accepting that degree from the President of the University was one of the proudest moments of my life. My smile was from ear to ear, and was broader than most anything on the horizon. But afterward, there was a problem.

"What am I supposed to do now?" I asked Jake. I wanted to continue on; I've always loved the challenges of school—learning, competing—but I was through with this particular journey.

"Why don't you go on to graduate school?" he replied, non-chalantly. I have to agree; the thoughts had always been there, and it was a forever wish. *I could do that, couldn't I?* When I was a teenager, I dreamt of getting my Ph.D. *Dr. Marley Thomson-(?)… I liked the sound of that.*

And that's what I did. I studied for the grueling entrance exam I had to take—and pass—in order to get into graduate school. It was horrible. A 4-hour test on things I had no idea even existed, but I did it, and I passed. Then, I was accepted into graduate school. *Wow! What a wish come true! Oh, what a feeling!*

Not only was I now in Graduate College, but I had recently been *successfully* (almost unheard of) released from the ten-year probation I had incurred *and* endured, and I was ecstatic! I was at the climax of life; it was MINE, and I was full of it! Finally, after all these years, it seemed like *everything* was on my side, and I had the world in the palm of my hand.

~✝~

Sissy and Mom and I took a summer trip to the mountains. The three-story log-cabin (or should I call it a mini-mansion?!) where we stayed offered the most gorgeous mountainous views of Pike's Peak on one side, and the precious village of Old Cripple Creek—*ah, memories of great times with my in-laws*—on the other. *God's land is so beautiful, isn't it!?* The weather was picture-perfect, and so was *most* of our stay.

We went white-water rafting, sight-seeing & hiking, and had a wing-ding of a time. And for the first time in my entire life, I went to a place where marihuana was legal. *Seriously!? Can life get any better than it is for me at this moment?!!* I was on top of the world—figuratively speaking, and literally.

This place was like a candy store for kids. Better yet, a toy-store for kids; a fucking (THC) candy-store for me! It was a damn marihuana retail store! I couldn't believe it was true. All I had to do was pick out the marihuana plant of my choice, pot-cookies, pixie-stix, lemon drops, gummy things…. whatever the hell I wanted, pay for it, and walk out the door—*legally!* I bought a bunch of THC goodies.

I was thinking that if I just stuck with smoking pot—I could do that now, since my ten-year supervised perdition with people I didn't know, was over—I wouldn't drink. *Just smoke pot, I told myself. It's a good high, a natural high, and I don't get soused.* I've never done anything violent or stupid from being "high", (except eat all of Sissy's wedding cake in the duration of a year, and stupid *little* shit like that), and I certainly don't have blackouts.

~✝~

Life was revved in 5th gear and I was enjoying the ride! When I got home from the mountains with Sis and Mom, it was going to be "all summer long in my backyard paradise with my Baby; graduate school and good living". I was stoked. But Jake had reservations.

"That shit's just going to get you into more trouble, Baby", he told me when I got back from vacation.

"Bullshit…it's going to keep me sober from drinking," I insisted.

"Baby-Doll, I sure hope you're right. Have fun with it, but be careful," he said.

CHAPTER 52

MY SMOKING AND NON-DRINKING PLAN lasted a whole minute. Sure, the pot was great—it always was for me. Always puts me in a good mood, never a foul one. And no paranoia here; not like it does to some people. In fact, I become energetic and useful when I'm "stoned"; productive, stuff like that.

~†~

The night was just a regular night, nothing fancy happening in our household. We both worked hard that day; I had neither class, nor homework. The bottle of wine was waiting for me when I got home, as usual. Jake had a beer or two by now. We tried to decide where we wanted to eat out; that's rarely an easy task for us.

"Where do you want to eat, Marley?" He asks every time.

"I don't know. Why do I always have to figure it out? Where do *you* want to eat, Jake?"

"Doesn't matter to me. Anything's fine. Wherever you want to eat, Baby. Just tell me where to go." By this time, we're in the car, and Jake is wanting a fast answer; he doesn't want to drive around town just to be driving—he's had a beer or two by now. *And it really sucks if he's headed the opposite direction from where I say to go.*

"Then at least tell me *what* you want to eat, and I'll say where." I at least try to be fair. "You're part of this twosome, Jake." I'm pretty aggravated by now. *We try to have date-night at least once a week, but there's no wonder it doesn't work out that way.*

This goes on for a while, and he gets pissed off because we're just "driving around". We are definitely quarreling.

"Oh, fuck it. Just go home. I don't even want to go out anymore." I hate this!

"C'mon, Marley, gawddamnit. We're going out to eat. You're always bitching because we never go anywhere, so where do you want to go?" he demands, and I cannot stand him at this point.

We end up at some establishment named after some dude, and we're both on a mission to enjoy the damned evening—or dinner, at least. Jake orders drinks for two.

By now, we've managed to get out of our "Where the fuck are we going to eat?" funk. However, I usually hold on to mine longer than he does. But, Jake always manages to get some laughter out of me at my most infuriated moments. We order dinner.

The atmosphere is pleasant, casual. Families and couples surrounding us, all seemingly having a nice time. We order more drinks. Our food comes.

I take a few bites, and decide I'll take the rest home. I'll eat it later.

"Here we go. Why the hell do we go out when you're always taking the shit home? What's the point?" *Jacob's forever argument.* He's being demanding, and I'm not about to hear it.

"What the hell do you care, Jake? Why does it bother you? The whole point is to get out of the house; let someone wait on us for a change. Enjoy some drinks, some food, and each other's company. But fuck it. Eat your own fucking dinner and leave me the hell alone. Shit." Now, it's on. This happens a LOT! About now is when he tells me to quieten my voice and quit cussing.

"I'll have one more," I smile and tell the waitress as I point to my glass; she passes by headed to another table. As far as Jake's concerned, I've committed adultery right before his very eyes, with no remorse in sight. The important thing at this point…I'm fucking pissed! *Ruin my night-out, why don't you?!*

"Why do you always do this, Jake? Why can't we just go out, have a nice time—you do your thing and me mine—together? Why do we always have to be in an argument *before* we choose a fucking restaurant? I hate this shit!"

Another one bites the dust. My spirit is broken, and so is date-night.

~✝~

"I'm going to bed," he says. Not a word was spoken on the ride back to the house. His image becomes smaller as he finds his way down the hallway, and disappears into the bedroom. Lights go out. *Asshole.* I went outside to take a few hits of my new "stash" …with my new pipe.

I sat under the light of the summer night's sky; it was the summer solstice. A dip in the pool would cool off my temper, maybe. It was worth a try, anyway. Afterward, I went to the store. I wanted more wine.

Actually, I did need things for the next day; I was giving a speech on something—I don't recall now—and I wanted to buy refreshments for my guests. The neighborhood store was just minutes away. Then, I wanted to find an open space that didn't have a fence around it; some place I could feel free without being "enclosed". Suburbia America always provided for an area park, open field or uninhabited meadow.

The sky was gorgeous, with its blue backdrop and violet reflections from the fiery pink sun. Rays of fuchsia and scarlet abound; I just wanted to sit and watch the glorious sunset before going back home. So, I did. And I basked in the moments of serenity that evening. I bathed my soul in the surroundings of peace.

PART IV:

CHAPTER 53

NO!! NO!! THIS CAN'T BE happening! It's a nightmare! It has to be a nightmare! Oh God, please let me wake up! Please, God… don't let this be happening!!

I shook and shook my head as if trying to get bugs out of my hair. I pinched myself and slapped my face over and over, trying to wake up from the surreal happenings. But I was still there. *Oh God, don't let this be true!*

The young Hispanic woman sharing the same 8x8 cinderblock room was hugging the wall opposite from where I was, at this point. She probably thought I was insane.

I could see men and women walking past the tiny square, plexiglass window the door provided. They were in brown uniforms, and I was in a holding cell—jail.

Just eight hours ago, I was sitting peacefully in a meadow next to a park. Birds were frolicking through the breeze and joggers were freeing their selves from stresses of the day before retiring for the evening. Cyclists were fulfilling their daily doses of adrenaline rush while children were swinging and dogs were catching frisbees.

The last thing I wanted to do was call home. But, it was also the *one* thing I wanted to do. *Jake. Oh, Jake.* I dreaded hearing his voice, but at the same time I needed to hear it. I needed my best friend, my rock, my soulmate—now more than ever before.

"Baby, where are you?! I've been worried sick! Are you in the hospital? Did you get arrested?" His voice was frantic, but with worry, fear. He was glad to hear mine.

When I said "Yes", he knew which question I was answering. I was sobbing, terribly, practically uncontrollably.

"I'm so sorry, Jake. I'm so sorry!" He could barely understand me.

"I've been worried sick about you! When you weren't in the house or the back yard, I went to the garage to see if your car was there. Oh God, I said…let her be all right." He hadn't slept for hours.

"I'll call the bondsman. I'll be there as soon as I can. Don't worry, Baby. It's going to be o.k., I promise." Jake was just glad I was all right. *He loves me so damn much!!!*

~†~

The magistrate reminded me of my Grandfather. He was an older man, and sort of kind…well, not really. *That's not why he reminded me of my grandfather; their looks were similar.*

This guy said, "Ma'am, do you know you're being charged with Driving While Intoxicated?"

"Yes sir," I responded, head down, feeling like the lowest, slimiest piece of shit that ever existed.

"It's a felony. Do you know that, too?" *Are you kidding me? This isn't my first rodeo, nor my second for that matter.*

"Yes, sir." Jeez, I hated to hear those words.

On the way out, the bondsman said to Jake, "This isn't her first rodeo…she knows the system."

I was feeling a sense of par amnesia—*deja-vu*. I was wishing I was in a real rodeo; riding my horse in a dirt-filled arena, wind in my hair, enjoying life the way I knew I could.

On the way to the wrecking yard to retrieve my precious small SUV, Jake was more solemn than I thought he would be. He was probably like me—in shock. But, I also guessed he was more relieved—than anything else—that I was at least alive. I was wishing I was dead.

Mexico is closer than Canada, and Mom hates to fly. It's cheaper, too. As a fugitive, I won't be able to afford much. Probably get some shit job somewhere and hole up in some shack near the ocean—that's the best I can expect, I'm sure. My thoughts were absolutely wild, unbelievable. *Will Jake come and visit me? Or will he leave me; will they all hate me, forever? 'Til death do us part, right? Oh God…I wish I was dead.* I would much rather be in heaven for all eternity, than in a prison cell for the remainder of my natural life.

CHAPTER 54

"THE LITTLE BLACK SUV THAT was brought in late last night?" The guy behind the desk looked at me like I'd turned into a fire-breathing dragon. He was quite unpleasant, to say the least. I was in no mood to put up with some jack ass's bullshit, asinine comments because of his bullshit, asinine, country-boy attitude.

"Yes, the black one. It's mine." I said as I stared, piercing him with dagger-rays.

"You're not going anywhere in that vehicle, Ma'am. It's totaled." Still, with his bull crap attitude.

Fuck! I didn't want to hear that! Marley, you didn't.

"You can get all your things out, though. Here's your key. It's on the first row, next to the Jag you totaled with it." This guy knew he was getting on my last fucking nerve. "Your insurance guy will be out within the next few days to assess their damages." *Crap! "Their" damages? That means it was "my" fault.* I seriously didn't think I could feel any worse than I was at this moment, but…

I almost raised my hands to the sky when I walked back outside. Not that I wanted God to lighten the tremendous load on my shoulders, but to pick me up and take me straight up to heaven. And, I wanted Jake to see where I was going. I was sure he was telling me—in his mind—to go straight to hell. Well, it was either jail or the grave for me in the near future, and I would much rather it be the latter; it sounded so much more inviting.

We retrieved what was left of my belongings in my now-pitiful used-to-be-beautiful SUV. I felt like I had deceived a friend and was leaving her to die. But my car had obviously already suffered what looked like a painful death.

I looked over at the other car I apparently "totaled". I prayed whoever was in that car, was all right.

The country-boy tow-guy gave me a copy of the police report. It had a diagram of the "collision", which included time and place of the accident. It was definitely my fault, but I had no recollection of being at that particular place the night before. It was in the opposite direction of the meadow; even going *away* from our home. *Where was I going? What was I doing there?* But, I did recall a harsh "jolt", and a loud noise.

"I thought you said you were… I thought you said you went to…" Jake kept asking questions, and I didn't have any answers. He wanted concrete, and all I had was zero.

"I'm trying to remember. Stop yelling at me!" But he wasn't yelling. It's just that any sound—from anyone or anything—was more than I could bear. I was racking my brain, trying desperately to remember what had taken place during those hours—those lost, eight hours.

~†~

I was crying so hard, trying to contain myself as I was explaining to my attorney my most recent legal, or should I say, illegal involvement.

By now, he'd become a real fixture in my life over the past fifteen years or so. He wasn't surprised—saddened, but not surprised. He'd come out of retirement for me any time—I was probably the one who allowed him to get to that point in the first place.

I sometimes picture him sipping umbrella drinks at his Caribbean Villa, with easy access to his very well-endowed bank account. Maybe he thanks me for his good-fortunes—my lack thereof. His gains are my losses. But, he's good at what he does and has helped me in the past. I needed him again.

"What?! How much?" I wanted to knock off some of the zeroes of the figure I was picturing in my mind. *Shit.*

I spent the rest of the day crying, in shock, and wishing life was over. I suppose it really was, in a way. We had already stopped by the store on the way home; I was in dire need of a major stress reliever.

~✝~

Work and school went along as scheduled. I looked at my coworkers, fellow-students and people on the streets and wondered if anyone had problems like I did. *Is there anyone here without faults, or failures?* I knew better, and I knew that everyone had skeletons in their closet, and yes, some worse off than me. And I knew that if anyone denied their skeletons, they were lying. Outright lying.

I prayed hard, very hard. All my life I've felt I've had a special relationship with my Lord and Savior, and now I was begging for His mercy. *Please, Lord…don't leave us now. Help us get through this one.*

Some of the intense emotional pain was stemming from knowing I'd have to come clean with my parents. How could I possibly break their hearts, again? After all I'd accomplished in the past few years—job, college degree, acknowledgements of being a pillar in my community, even graduate school—and now this.

I have always been my parents' "go to" girl. They could almost always depend on me for being there for them, for whatever reason. I always promised that I'd never live more than a weekend's drive away from Bridgeton, as long as Mom and Dad were alive. And now I was wishing I was dead; but that would kill them. *Even my choice of words sucked.*

Seems all I could do was cry. I was severely depressed, and trying to remain calm, with a sense of "normalcy", whatever that was at this time. But I told Mom and Dad, and like Jake, they were compassionate, understanding, and non-judgmental. They knew I had a "disease", and that it often got the best of me. Sure, they were deeply saddened, but very supportive.

I hated myself; I wanted to run away from *me*. Being in my own skin was horrible, but I was stuck with myself. And still, I was the luckiest person I had ever known.

~✝~

One of my bond requirements was to have an interlock device on my car, but *what* car? I didn't have one.

My claim was settled—I thought—and with the insurance money I received, I purchased a small sporty car, complete with sunroof and a few fun things like that. At least I could get to work and school, and maintain my routine stuff; do all the things a successful failure does in a somewhat normal life.

Then about a month after my wreck, I received a bill. It was for an emergency room visit, dated that dreadful night.

A day or two later, I received another bill. This time it was from the ER doctor. It too, was dated the night of my wreck. *Shit! What the hell has happened?!*

But the thing that truly floored me was when—that same week—I received an invoice from EMS; an ambulance bill. *Dear God…please help me to remember what happened that night!*

I called the ambulance company, and the hospital that sent the bill. Anything they could tell me was more than I already knew, or *didn't* know.

I tried to make it sound like I was in a state of shock that night, and had questions pertaining to the accident. I didn't want them to know I was in a blackout; that I couldn't remember anything about it.

I guess several months went by before the insurance claim was finally completed. I kept thinking what an idiot the insurance people must have thought I was; I was always adding bills, and asking weird questions. I remember being relieved when the claim was finally closed; one less thing to worry about.

CHAPTER 55

JUST MOMENTS AGO, OR SO it seemed, life was absolutely wonderful. My future was promising; looking to the future was exciting, even thrilling. Now, I asked myself if it was all over before it had gotten started. *What a damned idiot! What a stupid ass I am!* I could not believe this was happening, again. But, I was trying to remain positive and optimistic, staying busy with all my endeavors. Inside, I was dying.

My family, my God—they had all professed their forgiveness of this monumental screw-up. But forgiving myself wasn't an option. *What was wrong with them? What was wrong with me?*

"I'm Marley, and I'm an alcoholic." Attending AA meetings was part of the outpatient treatment I had checked myself into. My counselor was once a fellow-classmate who'd had his own brushes with the law—DWI's as well. *I should be on this side of the fence, not a client in rehab…again.*

"But she's a pillar of the community, look at her," David said as he pointed to me, looking at the other clients. I had come straight from work. Nicely dressed, highly-educated and well-mannered; sitting up in the chair with my legs crossed, hands folded and on my lap. Sweet, naïve David couldn't believe someone like me could possibly have problems with alcohol. I wasn't the stereo-typical, skid-row bum that so many people have in their image an addict. "Why are you here?" he asked.

"David, addiction doesn't show favoritism; it has no biases, no prejudices. On the inside, I'm just like you, or anyone else here in this group." The counselor had his eyes frozen on me. I was never sure why.

~†~

I did stop drinking, for a while. I wanted so badly to break away from the demons that bound me, and prove to myself, my family, and my God that I could live without alcohol. I wanted to give my body and soul a break. I was healthy in every way, except my mind. I wanted to relax; I wanted to drink.

I was smoking pot when I could, but that alone was short-lived. I had built up such a tumultuous, dysfunctional relationship with alcohol over the years, and I was missing my "best friend", as Jake called it. I insisted it was my "worst enemy".

I took pills to help me sleep, and Xanax to get me through the days. Trying like hell to focus on the generalities of life, but doing so was extremely hard. My thoughts were consumed with someone else deciding what my future would be, or not. I no longer had any control. I was scared to death, nervous, uneasy, and more than anything, angry. Then I'd take more pills to help me cope.

Often, I told Jake I understood if he left me; I'd leave me if I could. I didn't expect him to stay, but I wanted him to, naturally. I prayed for strength and perseverance. And I was drinking, more and more. My "devices" were helping me get through this incredibly dark time. Or were they?

Jake backed up this sick, totally fucked-up way of thinking. In fact, sometimes he encouraged it. I was certainly sick, but he was a co-inhabitant of my very disease; perhaps with just a less serious case.

CHAPTER 56

DURING THE TWO YEARS IT took from the time I had my wreck, was convicted and sentenced, Jake and I tried to live as normally as possible—whatever the hell that meant.

We took a couple of winter ski trips and the occasional beach trip, enjoyed our home and our lovely tropical backyard. And we enjoyed each other, *most* of the time.

I was trying not to drink, but ended up doing so more than ever, it seemed. Every time I'd insist on it NOT being in the house, *somehow* it made its way back in. Like a damn nasty rat, you can never get rid of! A pest; a nuisance. It was something I decided I truly didn't want, but Jake had another opinion.

"You're going to want it eventually, and I don't want to have to go back to the store every time you get in one of your 'moods'. Besides, you're going to have to quit soon anyway, so you might as well enjoy it while you can".

I needed him to understand me. I needed him to listen. I need him to help me. I needed him to know I was serious this time; but I was serious so many times before. My life was being broken into pieces, and if I had to separate from Jake to save myself, so be it.

~†~

We spent about two weeks looking at one-bedroom apartments, duplexes—whatever we could find that was small, and that we could afford. I'd already picked up the papers from my lawyer, and presented them to Jake. I needed him to know I was serious, now, more than ever. My drinking had to stop, and Jake was going to have to leave in order for me to do so. Ending the marriage to the man I cherished would tear me apart, but the alcohol was ruining my life; it was killing me. I gave him one month to find a place, and move out.

He first told me he wouldn't meet my "demands"; that he wouldn't quit drinking because of "your problem". I could quit, but, why should he? I told him it was no longer welcome in our home, and if he needed it, then neither was he.

"I can't lose you, Marley. I love you; I love our home. These places are depressing me terribly, and I hate the thought of us not being together. I've been thinking so hard, and you're right. I will stop drinking—at least at home, and in front of you. And I'll go to AA with you, or the other one, whatever you want me to do." *The proof is in the pudding my dear…the proof is in the pudding.*

~†~

"Hi. I'm Jake, and I'm an alcoholic." He was with me at *his* first AA meeting, and I couldn't have been prouder. We each received a "desire" chip, and met some real neat folks; I knew some of them already from my previous years there, and Jake really enjoyed the comradery, fellowship and genuineness amongst the members. I think he realized they were real people—just like us.

Our new lifestyle was short-lived. They say "you can't teach an old dog new tricks", but I say you can—only if he wants to learn. A few short months later, we were back to our old ways. Don't they also say "old habits are hard to break"?

I was about to lose my mind, and was sure of it. *Finally,* my grades were dropping drastically. I was worried and tired, and tired of worrying.

Court dates were received, and re-scheduled—time and time again. I was gaining weight from the stress, the lack of sleep, and the sauce. My psyche and emotional being were absolutely turbulent, and I was worn down. My spirit was broken and my soul was just lost. But I kept praying, constantly. The very few friends and family members who knew my situation prayed right along with me. *Thank you, all.*

CHAPTER 57

THE D.A.'S OFFICE HAD GONE from insisting I do ten years, to seven, to five. My lawyer knew I would never agree to five years in prison; he also knew he didn't want to refund any of the enormous chunk of change he'd been given—this time. He was fighting hard for me, and I trusted him. We also knew that a jury would throw the book at me; lock me up and throw away the key. So, we were settling for ten more years' probation. The very thought of it made me ill; the humiliation, the degradation, the fees, supervision, community service hours. And that's not counting all the extras I'd have to have; to pay for. But, the thought of being locked up in prison was worse. *Oh, if I could only have a "re-do" of that night. Just one night.*

Me and alcohol; alcohol and me. Two subjects destined by fate to be together in a dysfunctional, tumultuous and lethal relationship that never should have been. The allotment in life that proved over and over to be my misfortune.

One subject vulnerable to a lethal attraction, and the relationship begins. They start out having fun, getting their kicks. The seriousness takes over and the fighting begins. The desires persist, but the abuse prevails. The knock-down-drag-outs become a part of their normal routine; they have a love-hate relationship. The two are best friends and worst enemies, simultaneously. They break up for a moment but the bad memories subside, and before you know it, the pair is joined again. Only this time, they pick up where they left off. Their partnership in destruction only progresses each and every time; their sickness and dysfunction continues to metastasize. The only way out of this hellacious turmoil is through death, incarceration, or the decision to break free—once and for all. Me and alcohol. Alcohol and me.

~†~

I went to court knowing I'd come out, somewhat free. I'd be "supervised", once again, and for so very long, but at least I could finish school, keep what dignity I had left and strive forward with whatever integrity I managed to corral that was ingrained in me since childhood. I would work on my disconcerted state of being as well as my failing marriage, but at least I would have the opportunity to do so. I could build up my moral, engage in some sort of pride along the way, and implement the persona I so wanted for me. And I would try, like hell, to do it sober. But, that's not the way it happened.

"The D.A. has been looking over your history, Marley, and they will not grant probation. You can have a trial by jury, or five years' incarceration; you'll probably do two, or a little less." My lawyer's eyes had turned glossy. "I'm as surprised as you are, Marley. I'm so sorry."

Incarceration. Prison. Locked up. The "pokey". Penitentiary. Life, over.

He put his hand over mine, trying to console what he thought was coming; but nothing. I had no expression. I was in shock. There was a tear rolling down my cheek, off my jawbone, but I couldn't feel anything. I was numb.

"You've got to make a decision now, Marley. What are you going to do?" I didn't like my choices.

I knew a jury would lynch me and leave me for the buzzards, unanimously. Their decision would probably make me happy with the ten-year sentence the D.A. originally offered. I took the five years; I signed on the dotted lines.

When my brain began to function again, besides my family, my life, and my freedom, I could only think about school. I wanted desperately to at least finish out the semester; I couldn't screw *that* up, too. The investment—both timewise and financially, I needed to finish what I'd started. I was granted four weeks to finish out the six-week semester. At least I could work it out with my professors with *some* dignity and whatever energy I could muster up before I was forced to turn myself in.

I walked out of the courthouse, and although I was dying inside, I held my head up high, breathed in the fresh air, and looked toward the blue sky. As I was getting in my car to go home, I was wishing I was climbing into the back of a hearse.

~✝~

Jake and I spent the evening crying—me more than him, of course. He held me and tried to console me as much as possible. We tried to come up with reasons why the five years was better than ten years' probation, and of course, the jury trial.

"You'll be out before you know it, Baby; maybe a year and a half, two years at the very most. We'll be fine. No more of that probation bullshit, and you'll be free. You'll be fine. We'll be fine. I love you so much, Marley. And we'll be through…never, never again." Jake was so sincere, and sounded so positive, even at this lowest, awful moment.

Just a couple of years of my life; that's all they could have from me. Sure, I'd do some time in prison, then finish the rest on paper. That's what kept me hopeful—knowing I'd have a chance at an early release—parole. With my background of successful probation and rehab, surely, they'd let me out on my first parole hearing—*I hoped*. But right now, I was scared to death, and wishing it was all over before it'd even begun. Four more weeks of freedom, sort of. *I can do this; I have to do this. I am woman…hear me roar. meow.*

Jake and I spent the next few hours cuddled on the sofa by the fireplace…Jake knew a fire in the fireplace would put my mind at ease; soothe my disenchanted soul. He knew I needed all the soothing I could get.

He smiled, even chuckled at my pathetic appearance as I told him what all had transpired that day. But I knew he was fighting back his tears, so that mine could flow. He knows my heart and was feeling my pain.

CHAPTER 58

(ONE MONTH LATER…) JAKE KISSED me like he'd done the very first time he kissed me, so many years ago. We held hands, squeezing our interlocked fingers together as if making a chain that would prove by any strength to be unbreakable. And we hugged, and hugged…and hugged.

The console was between us, and I told him there was no reason for him to go in with me. I wasn't coming out, not with him anyway, and I didn't want him coming back out of the courthouse by his self, feeling sad, lonely, lost. I just wanted him to drop me off, and be on his way.

"I love you, Jake. I love you with all my heart. And don't forget to pray. Pray hard, every day. Be strong Baby, and pray. Don't forget how much I love you…and don't forget to pray." I was trying with all my might to hold back the tears. I wouldn't allow it.

"I love you so much, Marley! You'll be home before you know it. You can do this, Baby. You've got this, and I've got you. I love you, Baby." Jake was holding back his tears, too. "Call me as soon as you can."

He watched me walk until I was out of sight, and inside the courthouse. *What horrible, empty, useless feelings we were both having. Such a very sad day.*

~✝~

The judge wished me luck, and I was escorted by a guy in a uniform to a back room—me and a few other people. Like a criminal, I was handcuffed, shackled, and helped up into the back of what looked like an armored car. I couldn't figure out if I was being protected, or protected from.

The next few weeks were awful, but if I had been a fortune-teller, I would have been grateful for what I had there, and at the time; what I had coming would be the worst days of my life, and then some.

The time I spent in county jail was considered baby steps toward the full-fledged journey to hell I experienced in state prison. I never knew life as a human being could be so humiliating, so menial, and downright degrading. I hated this place and everyone in it. It was a melting pot of ethnicities, cultures, and a huge array of heathens; some human, many probably not. I had never known such stink or ugliness like I experienced every day. I would have rather taken my chances at a zoo; living in a cage with wild lions, crazy apes and man-eaters. Never had I known a place where so many diverse, mixed up, confused, mean and lost souls perpetrated daily. And I was there with them. I hadn't forgiven myself until now, but now I did. I had to; I was all I had and my only friend. *I am here, until God says otherwise.* I knew that, and I trusted it. I had to make peace with myself and where I was, because I knew that the coming days would only get worse.

I prayed constantly, for peace and patience, as I sat amongst the confines of concrete cinder blocks and the coldness of steel. The harshness of the metal doors with their constant banging and clanging; it was the sound only one should experience in a nightmare, and this was my reality. Everyone around me was rude, ruthless, non-caring and ignorant. Many didn't give a damn about their selves and certainly not anyone else. Some didn't even know how to care, even if they so desired. Not only the inmates around me, but the guards as well. *Are they actually people? Humans?* Their skin was steel-wool and their insides were rotten. They were the rejects of their own hay-day, and this was where life had taken them- to care for the demons within these pathetic walls. I had to pray for all of us.

Some people belong here; many do not. There are those who have lived their lives in the prison of addiction; a life of misery and failure without any hope of redemption. Addictions of not only alcohol and drugs, but of immoral sexual behaviors and indecisive sexual preferences, gambling and theft, and shit you'd never imagine. Some people are just addicted to hopelessness and destruction of life. Many have been here before, and many have not. As for me, never again will I give the devil his due.

I was disgusted by the unjust I saw. I didn't know third world wrong existed in my own country, in my own "backyard". Months in this prison hell and all I could see was a black hole; no light at the end of anything; not even a flicker. All I could fathom was a dark alley-way, which filled me with fear. I was lonely and exhausted, and I wanted to go home. I wanted Jake to hold me; *let me close my eyes and bury my head in his loving arms while he caudles me, and I wrap my body up in a ball, into the fetal position of safety and security.*

I was sick of the lesbian orgies and humping contests going on in the bunk beside me, or the one beside that, or across the hallway. I couldn't stand the sight of women fighting, clawing at each other until their eyeballs bled, while the guards looked away. Sometimes they'd watch a while, then look away. They didn't care. I didn't want to hear any more; see anymore. I was sickened to my soul and didn't know how much more I could take, seriously. *It isn't right; it isn't normal, and it's everywhere I turn. Just put me in solitary confinement, please.* And so, it was.

I was taken out of the malignant environment I had lived in for months, to a place I *thought* was going to be somewhat better. But I questioned my thoughts after being rustled like cattle—with a load of stinking filth—into what looked like an old freight container used by the first railroads built in the 1860's. Had I been in purgatory and now going to hell? Or was I going from hell #1 to hell #2?

The parole officer I was interviewed by said to me, "Good people don't belong here. Do what you can to get out, and never come back." He also said to me, "DWI...alcohol. Hmm...I can always tell," while he looked me over as if trying to figure out where he was going to take the first bite. *What the fuck did that mean? Because I have all my teeth?* I took it as a compliment, if it was an insane possibility.

He explained to me the virulent atmosphere he had witnessed over the years while working in the deadly hell of the prison system. It wasn't good, and we both wanted me out of there.

The place I was taken to was to be a ship passing through the night, only the ship was worse than the undignified piece of third-world hell I'd just come from, and the night lasted for over two months. I was in solitaire, waiting, and waiting. It was an even more dungenous hell than I had been privy to, and I thought things couldn't get worse.

What privileges I had before—if that's what you want to call them—were all taken away. I couldn't call Jake, at all. At least in the previous place I could use the phone. I couldn't hear for the racket and yelling constantly going on, but at least there was some sort of connection with my outside world. I couldn't watch a television; there wasn't one. And I couldn't read a book; I had my library privileges taken away. Had the parole officer been being facetious while interviewing me? What had I done that I couldn't talk to my husband, couldn't watch the news of the outside world, couldn't read a book that put me miles away from my harsh reality? I hadn't gotten any cases, as most people do, sometimes daily. I stayed away from the riots, the fights, the bullshit—well, as much as I could. What was going on, I wondered? Why have they put me here, away from everyone and everything? I had wished for isolation, and now, very eerily, I had it.

I didn't see the sky, or a blade of grass for months. I was in a tiny, old, nasty cell in an ancient, decrepit structure of what was supposed to be a building. The plumbing was probably the original; put in eighty years ago when the rock-house was built. I sat, and sat, and sat, watching the cockroaches, waiting for someone to tell me why I was there. The only thing I knew was that I was in "transition." Women all around me came and went, but I remained. I kept praying I wasn't lost in the system.

I was allowed three meals a day; ten minutes each. Even the every-other-day, five-minute shower I was allotted was behind a locked, barred door. *This isn't right. I'm trying to do better, and everything's getting worse. I'm a far cry from a deranged killer or a serial rapist.* I tried desperately to hold on to the tiny bit of self-worth I had left. I wasn't about to give the devil any more pleasure at my expense—*Hi, I'm Marley. I'm an alcoholic. I'm finally that skid-row bum.* And when no one would give me an answer, I just waited…and prayed. *Patience and peace, God. Please give me patience and peace.*

I knew of one particular verse in the Bible, and I prayed it constantly: "Wait patiently for the Lord. Be brave and courageous, yes, wait patiently for the Lord." *Psalm 27;14.*

And then one morning, very early before dawn, everything changed.

CHAPTER 59

CHAINS WERE PUT AROUND MY waist, with chains attaching my handcuffs to my shackles, I was taken with a few other women and loaded into a van. *Where are we going this time? What's going on?* Little did I know I was granted parole. But before I could go home, I had to complete a very *extended* rehab program—one that would last many months. It was strictly for women who were in prison for offenses such as mine, women who had made a serious mistake—sometimes the same one, over and over. It was for women who had committed the crime in their addiction with no malicious intent, never meaning to harm anyone. Unforeseen crimes, but crimes all the same.

The drive was lengthy, and about the time the sun was coming up, we drove into the parking lot of the place where I would spend the remaining era of my prison journey. I had heard about this place, and it was all decent, at least as far as prison goes, if that's possible. A "private prison", they called it.

"They call this the Princess' Prison," one fellow joy-rider said.

"Yeah, and I've heard it called 'camp cupcake'," another said. "At least it's not the state-run bullshit we just came from. Thank you, Lord," she said, as she looked toward the roof of the van.

"We're here, ladies." The driver said; I thought I'd died and gone to prison purgatory. *Did that guy seriously just call us "ladies"? Wow! That's a first in all my months of incarceration.* He got out of the van, and began to help us out, one by one.

The inside of "camp cupcake" was like a high-school—women walking the halls to and fro, carrying books, chatting to one another *and* laughing with staff—*guards*. I felt like I was in a Twilight Zoned movie staged in a women's college somewhere off in time. And they all had on outfits of various colors. Some women were in yellow, some in pink; others in blue, and some in Aggie maroon. I couldn't believe what I was seeing. And the walls! The walls were painted beautifully, murals everywhere, with positive affirmations, Bible verses…optimism abound. I guess I thought I'd died and gone to prison-heaven.

I walked in my assigned dorm, and received a half-ass standing ovation, with women smiling, clapping, coming over to welcome me. The place was clean, decent, and cool. And after I settled in, someone hollered, "Rec!"

I was invited along by a fellow "dorm-mate", and to my surprise, the outside yard was huge, with a running/walking track around the perimeter of the grass-covered lawn, and an area where a tall pavilion was providing shade to a large array of weights and workout equipment. I looked around and saw women laughing and playing volleyball with their shoes off and toes in the sand. They were actually having fun. And I heard music. On another side of the tremendous yard I could see women exercising to the beat of salsa music, like I used to do in Zumba classes. *That's what they're doing…they're doing Zumba!* I was in awe, and amazed. I was glad to be where I was, and not glad to be where I was. *I will make the best of this, and I will go home, a better person.*

~✝~

I settled in my dorm room which resembled greatly a regular college dorm room. I had a roommate, my own space—tiny as it were, but mine all the same—and a bit more peace than I previously held. I went to church regularly, attended AA meetings several times a week, signed up for retreats and random activities, and eventually sang in the choir. I walked five miles a day and worked out consistently. I became healthier than almost ever.

My days consisted of therapy—group, individual, and various "themed" classes with licensed counselors. We even had a Warden who showed compassion, empathy, and concern for everyone he encountered during his daily walks throughout the facility. And he always had a friendly "Hello," accompanied with a smile.

I didn't know privileges like this existed in prison life; certainly not in the places I had been. I felt bad for the women left behind, and I prayed for them. I prayed for me; I prayed for my family. I prayed for every individual I met, didn't meet, and didn't want to meet. Sure, there were undesirables there, but don't they exist everywhere in life? Isn't that what I had become in my own insignificant existence?

I pondered, and prayed. I tried to analyze a deeper meaning of my incarceration, and my life's experiences. Being all too familiar with the cliché "*There's a reason for everything…*" I, too, held that motto close to my bosom. I've believed in that phrase whole-heartedly, and always. But it took on a much more potent meaning to me now, and here.

My compassion literally cries out to help others in need. Sometimes I want to wave a magic wand at someone else's woes, and change their frowns to laughter. Problems aren't always solvable, but I wear my toolbelt of empathy, sincerity, and the desires to comfort and be supportive to others. I don't always succeed, but I usually try.

Has my perpetual calling landed me here not only for myself, but to help another woman who faces her future with my same burdens? I believe our earthly existence is to help each other get from this life to the next… Is this my present destiny?

Is my addiction a façade to mask my true identity? Is it a part of me so I can share experiences giving what I know to others who suffer from such afflictions? Is it God's intent for me to know hands-on, the depth of the agony and destruction my addiction purposes? Am I being punished for my sinful nature, but consequently developing a knowledge of how to help save what could be someone else's inevitable tragedy, or even demise? Do the insufferable hours I spend here compare to what I should be doing in the free world?

Have I not heard enough of people's dysfunctional lives, filled with trauma, deceit, pain and misery to write the tales of a lifetime? I've heard numerous stories of immoral despair; I've been told of incest and heartache, rape and death, within the most rage-filled rants. Stories of sorrow, penance, neglect and ignorance. The tellers of these tales express their words with tears, and sometimes a sobbing cry—like that of a mother in mourning for her lost child.

I've opened my ears to women pouring out their deepest fears. I've even heard some repent for their sins to me, as if I were the one offering absolution. I've heard words of sorry and regret, and promises of future intent. And I've wiped the tears of many, including my own.

I've listened to loneliness and have begged for God's mercy. We've sought out reasons for our destruction and prayed for recovery. Some of these women have become my friends; they have a place in my heart.

We are wives, daughters, mothers, sisters, and friends. We are someone's aunt, niece and grandchild. We are someone's grandparent, or God-parent. We are someone's cousin, and a neighbor.

We are someone who allowed the devil to creep into the tiny crack of our souls that had come loose after stretching ourselves too thin. We lost a part of God's glue that held our souls together, allowing the demon to slither in at our most vulnerable moments. For that moment—stolen from Satan and lost to us—we are here to pay the price. But, we are that good person—the loving mother, the proud wife, the devoted daughter. We are the good neighbor and the caring friend. We're the Christian who loves God and accepts Jesus as our Lord and Savior.

Our lives will mend and move forward from where we sit. We aren't bound for a life of hell. This is our life—my life, and I won't allow the Devil to use it for his entertainment, not any more. Not through a crack in my soul or a hole in my heart; I will be whole…I will be complete.

I will break free from the chains that not only bind me in this or any physical damnation—places of bedlam, but internally—in my mind and my heart—I will be imprisoned, no more.

EPILOGUE

(MONTHS LATER...FINALLY AT HOME) "OH Jake! It's so good to be home! I can't believe I'm finally back home...That hell is so fucking over! I missed you so much. Baby, I can't thank you enough for being there, here, for me, and never leaving my side. I witnessed so many sad situations as marriages, relationships were torn apart. But we're so strong, and I'm so blessed. It was horrible for me, yes, but I know it was so tough on you. I'm so sorry, Baby. I'm so sorry." Tears were welling up, *again,* as we laid on the bed, wrapped in each other's arms, savoring every precious moment together. The day was absolutely beautiful!

"Our lives start anew, Marley. Right now. Sober, and happy. Free, and together. I love you, Baby, more than anything. Didn't we vow, 'til death do us part? For better *or* worse? But NEVER again, Marley, never again." We were eye-to-eye, and he was serious. Jake wiped my tear. "Come here, gorgeous..." Grabbing, groping, hugging...he was smiling that glorious smile at me.

We laughed and made love for days.

~†~

"I hate to do it, but you know I've got to go back to work Monday. I want you to just settle in, take it easy, get acclimated to being back home. Sleep late, swim...have some fun, honey, and enjoy being home. Take a few months off before deciding what you really want to do. There's no rush, Baby."

"I do have meetings I need to go to, and I want to do some visiting... go hang with Mom and Dad, sort of catch up on stuff. Oh, and I want to get started on my walks at the park. And, I've been thinking. You know, Jake...I think I'll write a book."

Note to readers: If you or a loved one suffers from exposure to addiction of any form, I urge you to seek help. As stated in the dedication, there are plenty of resources available to those affected. Please contact your local Alcoholics Anonymous, Al Anon, Narcotics Anonymous, Gamblers Anonymous, or alcohol and drug abuse prevention coalition(s). Whatever your addiction, whether first or second-hand, please, seek help. It's there for the taking. Thank you.

Printed in the United States
By Bookmasters